'You'd better be with us, Nora,' Damien said.
'If you're not with us you're against us.'
'I'm not with anybody,' I said.
'Right!' he said. 'Then nobody's with you. Nobody will speak to you or have anything to do with you, Nora-No-Guts, because you are a coward and a traitor!'

Colum stuck out his tongue at me. James Rice spat at my feet. He wiped his mouth with the back of his hand and blew a raspberry in my face. Then he gave me a look and walked away.

It hurt to be called Nora-No-Guts and to have no one speak to her at school but Nora saw no point in the fight with the Gobbers . . .

Island of the Strangers

CATHERINE SEFTON

Mammoth

For Queenie Pinnons

First published in Great Britain 1983
by Hamish Hamilton Children's Books
Magnet paperback edition published 1984
Published 1990 by Mammoth
an imprint of Mandarin paperbacks
Michelin House, 81 Fulham Road, London SW3 6RB
Reprinted 1991 (twice)

Mandarin is an imprint of the Octopus Publishing Group

Text copyright © 1983 Catherine Sefton

ISBN 0 7497 0182 X

A CIP catalogue record of this title
is available from the British Library

Printed and bound in Great Britain by
BPCC Hazell Books
Aylesbury, Bucks, England
Member of BPCC Ltd.

"You'd better be with us, Nora," Damien said. "If you're not with us, you're against us."

"I'm not with anybody," I said.

"Right!" he said. "Then nobody's with you. Nobody will speak to you or have anything to do with you, Nora-No-Guts, because you are a coward and traitor!"

One

"Nora! Nora!"

Orla Donnelly came in through our back window, whooping my name at the top of her voice. She landed in the dog basket, and almost killed our cat. Our cat Leary sleeps in the dog basket and our dog Erk mostly sleeps on my little brother Chris.

"Nora-Nora-Nora!" Orla gabbled, all oyster-eyed. She often gabbles like that when she has something to say which she thinks is exciting.

"What-what-what?" I said, not to be outdone.

"There are a lot of wild kids wrecking Egg's Shop!" Orla announced, bouncing out of the dog basket and, at the same time, helping herself to my second last piece of toasted soda bread and a big dollop of Stella's homemade strawberry jam.

"If you eat all my breakfast, I will fade away to nothing," I said, removing the plate and the last piece of soda bread from her reach.

"Mrs. McEntee says I've got to build myself up," Orla said, munching happily. I don't know where she puts it. She is a titch with a mop of red hair stuck on top.

"They-they-they . . ." Orla was off again, eyes glistening with excitement.

"They *what*?" I said, impatiently. Orla would go on for ever if you let her. She is quite a sensible person when she calms down, but when she gets excited anything can happen.

"They got out of their bus and they are running round on the shore thumping each other and some of them went into Mrs. Egg's shop and now she is having a row with the beardy man and — do-you-want-that-apple?"

"What beardy man?" I asked, letting her take the apple. It was easier than watching her mope if I said "no".

"The beardy man who came with them. He has a black beard and a funny hat. Mrs. Egg chased three of them out of her shop and now the man is yelling at them and Mrs. Egg is shouting at him and the kids are all over the place."

"I'm going to see this!" I said.

We went down the lane toward Egg's Corner to see what it was all about. I walked and Orla bounced, which is her normal way of getting about. I thought that Orla was making some of it up. Stella says Orla has more imagination than is good for her.

This time it wasn't all Orla's imagination.

There were about thirty kids in denims down on the shore, and parked by the lamppost at

Egg's Corner was a minibus with 'Gobelier Street School Natural History Project' written on a blue card in the window and 'GOBBER RULE' written in the dust on the side. The beardy man was there, talking to Mrs. Egg. He had a tweed hat, with a feather.

"Told you!" Orla said, squeezing my apple with her palms to soften it.

"How're your teeth?" I asked, noticing what she was doing. She had wobbly teeth and they'd been hurting her.

"Dentist, *again*," she said, making a face.

"You haven't seen our Chris, have you?" I asked, turning my attention back to the Gobbers. Chris is my little brother. I didn't want him mixed up with a tough lot like that.

"He was throwing stones for Erk, down at Slaughter Point," Orla said, and then she added, "Mrs. Egg isn't being cross any more. You missed it!"

I knew why Mrs. Egg was behaving herself, even though the Gobbers were running about as though they'd just been let out of prison. Most of them were down on the shore, where they were stuffing seaweed down the neck of a skin head Gobber, but the beardy man had three of them working. He had bought a load of groceries from Mrs. Egg, and the Gobbers were carting the boxes to the bus. No wonder Mrs. Egg was looking pleased.

3

"Enough to feed an army," Orla said.

"Some army!" I said.

I didn't like the look of the Gobbers. They came in all sizes, and some of them looked pretty tough.

Egg's Shop is our General Store and the only shop there is round Leary's Lane and the Headland. It is the sort of shop where you can buy almost anything and get a talking newspaper as well, for Mrs. Egg has a lot to say for herself.

She does most of her talking in the summer when visitors come to look for bloodstains at Slaughter Point, but not many visitors come in October and take half the shop away in one visit.

We didn't go down to the Corner. Instead we got up on the sea wall and watched what the Gobbers were doing on the shore.

"*Trippers!*" Orla said, scornfully. She had no need to say it so loudly. Some of them heard her and they stopped trying to stuff seaweed down the skin head Gobber's neck. They came over and stood beneath us, looking up, as if we were monkeys in a zoo.

"What are they staring at us for?" Orla said, between munches of my apple. "They're very rude!"

"We were staring at them first," I said, and I hopped down off the wall.

I knew the danger signs. Orla didn't like them. She was getting mad.

A big Gobber shouted at Orla, and Orla took what was left of my apple and threw it at him. She missed, but that didn't matter. It was chucking the apple that counted.

The next minute they were pelting us. Sand, sticks, seaweed, even stones. The only good thing was that they were twenty feet beneath us and on the other side of the wall. Orla jumped off the wall and crouched down beside me.

"Keep your head down, Orla!" I shouted, and we crouched there, with half the beach flying over our heads. Orla started scrabbling around for things to throw back.

"Don't, Orla!" I said.

"What's wrong with you?" she said. "I'm only chucking back what they've chucked up."

She didn't manage to do it, however, for at that moment a white plastic shopping bag came whooshing up over the wall. It was a water bomb, and it drenched Orla.

"Augh!" Orla spluttered, angrily.

Then we heard the beardy man yelling.

"Run, Orla, or he'll get us," I said, and off we headed, up the lane. The next thing would be that he'd catch us and we would be dragged down to Mrs. Egg and she would tell Stella and Mrs. Donnelly and we would be in real trouble.

"Nip in the school, Orla!" I told her, and we

went in through the gate of our school, which is Ballyhannis School.

"You're a great one for running away," Orla said, splodging along beside me as we went round the back of the bike shed, which is our usual hiding place. The bins are there, and you can get down behind them. I was worried about Orla's drips giving us away, for she left a line of them behind her. We stayed crouched down behind the bins for a long time and nobody came, so we came out again to see what was happening.

The Gobbers had been marshalled into a queue to get back on to their bus, and the beardy man was marching up and down yelling at them. He got them on to the bus, then he counted them again and then he shut the door. He sat down in the driver's seat and the bus gave a rumble and moved off.

The man in the bus did a wild thing. Instead of driving his bus up the lane and along to the Field Centre on the Portmannis Road he drove straight past the lamppost and down round the side of the shop, on to the beach! There he revved up the engine and ploughed along the soft sand. The next thing we knew he was heading for the causeway.

The island opposite us, Inishnagal, is only just an island, for when the tide is low you can cross to it along the causeway with your shoes around

6

your neck. When the tide is high you could get drowned.

The tide was coming in, but it was Inishnagal he was making for.

"They'll get stuck," I said, watching the Gobbers' bus as it rocked and jolted and splashed along the causeway, with the water white against its wheels as the waves came. It is an old Poor Law Relief Work causeway, made in the nineteenth century when everybody was starving, and it is beginning to come to bits. I thought the minibus might stick in one of the holes.

It didn't and we had to do without the pleasure of watching the Gobbers swim for it in their denims. Instead the bus lurched over the old stones and the sandy bits where the sea has pulled the causeway apart, and jolted off on to Inishnagal itself, where it gave Mr. Cully's sheep a scare. They are used to having the island all to themselves in autumn, give or take a dead Spaniard.

There were lots of dead Spaniards there; first of all a whole lot of them were drowned when their boat caught on the Gull Cliff at the far end of the island, and then the ones that survived were put to the sword by Owen Leary.

Owen Leary is our local hero. He went round killing people. He pretended to be friendly to the Spaniards and he lured them off the island to a feast, and then when he got them down to Slaughter Point he put them to the sword. Afterwards he threw all the bodies into the sea. One of the Spaniards got away and fled back to the island. Owen Leary's men went after him and they had him trapped at the top of the Gull Cliff. The thing they didn't know was that the Spaniard was a witch! He turned himself into a gull and flew over their heads crying at them, calling on the souls of the dead Spaniards, and the next thing was that Owen Leary's men heard the dead Spaniards sighing at them, and they got off the island double quick! That is why the island is called 'Inishnagal' which means, Island of the Strangers.

"What are they going out there for?" Orla asked. We had climbed on to the roof of the bicycle shed to get a better view. The bus had stopped and the Gobbers were spilling out of it.

"Camping?" I suggested.

If there was a storm they would have their work cut out finding decent shelter. The island is mostly jagged rock, with a greenish bit at one side near the far end, running up towards the top of the Gull Cliff. The only shelter on the island is up there. It is supposed to be the ruin of a house the Spaniards made, but our teacher Mrs. McEntee says it is older than that. She says the Spaniards just used it because it was there, and because they thought it would be easy to defend. It is set in against the crumbly rocks at the top of the Gull Cliff, facing the land.

"They'll get no shelter in the Spaniards' House," I said.

"They could put a roof on," Orla said.

"I wouldn't fancy it."

"I would! We could do it sometime. We could . . ."

"No we couldn't!" I said, flatly.

"Why not?"

"Because I don't like the island," I said.

"You're afraid of cold dead Spaniards coming drip-drip-dripping up the Gull Cliff all wet and drowned."

"Don't be silly," I said.

"If you listen hard, you can hear the Spaniards sighing!" she said.

She thought she was very funny. She was remembering the time we went over to the island to see the Spaniards' House with Mrs. McEntee. Our whole class went and we thought we might find Spanish doubloons or gold, but we didn't. Mrs. McEntee said Owen Leary and his men would have looted anything that escaped the wreck. Then Sally Colley said she heard the Spaniards sighing one time, and half of the kids believed her and Mrs. McEntee was very cross because Damien Hughes started carrying on saying he was a witch. Mrs. McEntee says the

Spaniard wasn't a witch, he just hid somewhere, but we all looked for where he hid and we couldn't find it.

The island is a funny place. I wouldn't go there at all if it wasn't for the blackberries. We all go over for the blackberries because they are the best for miles. We have bramble jelly and blackberry crumble and the house smells of blackberry for weeks.

"Come on!" I said. "Let's go down to Egg's."

I went off down the lane to Mrs. Egg's shop to find out was happening. Orla came after me making jokes about drowned Spaniards.

"Are they going to camp on the island?" I asked Mrs. Egg.

"So the man says," said Mrs. Egg. "God help his wit! He had his Natural History Club booked in at the Field Centre, and the idea was to go down to the island. Now with the trouble at the Centre he says he's going to stay out there instead. Says it'll teach them what outdoor life is all about. Teach them! A pack of city savages like that! We'll all be murdered in our beds."

"Nobody's murdering me!" said Orla.

"I saw you give as good as you got," said Mrs. Egg, approvingly. I thought she might have told us off for fighting, but then she never takes to strangers, and her son Brendan is even worse! If Brendan had been hanging about our fight would have become a battle royal!

"Only four of them in my shop at a time, from now on, I told him," said Mrs. Egg. "Four at a time, for I don't want them wrecking the place."

"They'll be over four-at-a-time – if the tide lets them," I said.

We were all thinking the same thing. Inishnagal was a rotten place to dump a pack of city kids, especially in October with the tides running.

"What if it rains on them?" Orla said.

"Then they'll get wet, won't they?" said Mrs. Egg. She gave us one of her bright, birdy looks, and wagged her small head like a worm hunter. She is not as soft as she looks, Mrs. Egg. She is hard boiled. Hard-Boiled-Egg. That is one of my Egg jokes.

We got out of the shop and were on our way up the lane talking about the Gobbers and Mrs. Egg when suddenly something clicked in my mind.

"Our blackberries!" I said.

"What about our blackberries?"

I explained it carefully to Orla. Our blackberries were up around the Spaniards' House.

"The Gobbers are going to stuff themselves with all our blackberries!" I told Orla. "They're bound to go up to the Gull Cliff and then they'll find the blackberries and we will have no jam this year."

"We've got to stop them!" Orla said.

"Oh yes!" I said. "Sure!" Then I pointed out that the Gobbers were much bigger than we were, and probably tougher.

"I'm going to stop them just the same!" Orla said.

Two

"We're going to sneak over tonight and pick all the blackberries before the Gobbers find them!" Orla announced.

"I don't want to go," I said.

"Because you're afraid of the gull ghosts," Orla said.

"Nora's afraid of the ghosts!"

"Nora always was yellow!" said Brendan Egg. He is seventeen and he has left school and he hasn't got a job and he is the only one of his age left around here and he just loves trouble. I suppose it gives him something to do.

"I am not yellow, Brendan Egg!" I said, indignantly.

"Then you're coming with us," Brendan said.

I didn't like the way he had taken over the expedition all of a sudden, but I wasn't going to let him say I was yellow.

"All right," I said. "But no fights!"

I know Brendan. If he started imagining he was Owen Leary and fighting the Gobbers Stella would hear about it, and I would get into trouble for fighting and for being on the island after dark.

"I'll go if Stella lets me," I said.

"You're not going to tell Stella," Orla said, flatly. "You're not going to tell Stella because your Stella wouldn't let any of us go."

"Nobody'd stop me!" said Brendan.

"You're all right. You're big," said Orla. "But if she tells Stella nobody else will get going."

There aren't many kids round the Headland. There are only fourteen seniors at Ballyhannis school and of those only the Rices and Damien Hughes would be likely to go off on Orla's expedition. I might even have been able to talk her out of it if Brendan hadn't intervened.

"You're just using Stella as an excuse to get out of it!" Orla said.

"I'm not!"

In the end, I couldn't tell Stella. Instead I left a note on my bed with 'TO BE OPENED IF WE DO NOT RETURN' written on the envelope. In it I told Stella that we had gone on an after-dark blackberry expedition.

"It feels like cheating Stella," I said.

"You've done it now," said Orla, not caring a bit if I had cheated Stella.

Stella is our aunt. She looks after us because my mother is dead. She is not our real aunt, but my father's umpteenth cousin, three hundred times removed, on his mother's side. The arrangement is that Stella looks after me and Chris, and meantime she is doing her thesis. Ballyhannis is not the best place to be doing a thesis, and she finds it difficult to do with us to look after.

I knew it would be all right if my father could get the job that was going at the Field Centre or some other job near home instead of having to travel all the time. Until he could work something out, he paid Stella to look after us, and that was a great help to Stella, because she had no money and the Board kept mucking about over giving her a proper grant.

We met at Slaughter Point at half past seven, when we'd had our teas. In the end there were only four of us: Orla and me and Brendan and Damien Hughes. The Rices couldn't come because they had to help at home.

"Everybody ready?" Brendan said.

Everybody was.

"Don't go dashing on to the island, waving your buckets about," Brendan said. "Remember the Gobbers may have look-outs posted, and we don't want them to see us."

"Sounds like a replay of World War II!" I said to Orla, but she was looking very impressed.

"The girls go first," said Brendan.

"Oh *great*!" I said.

"They won't suspect anything if they see two little kids like you," Brendan explained. I felt like telling him that I wasn't a little kid and I wasn't taking his rotten orders, but in the end I didn't.

Off we went along the beach towards the causeway and the first person we bumped into was the last one we wanted to meet. It was Mrs. McEntee, our teacher.

"Orla Donnelly and Nora Mullan!" she said. "What are you two doing, all dressed up with your buckets?"

She was down on the shore paddling. No one else from round here goes paddling in October. Our sea is a cold sea. She goes swimming in winter and it turns her blue. If you ever see a frozen teacher floating past inside an iceberg it is our Mrs. McEntee.

"Blackberrying, Miss," Orla said, and I gave her a dirty look. She should have kept her mouth shut about the blackberrying in case Mrs. McEntee started asking if our people had given us permission.

"It is a bit late in the evening to go blackberrying, isn't it?" Mrs. McEntee said, landing on the weak spot straight away, as usual.

I could have told her it was a bit late in the year to be paddling on the shore, but I didn't. I kept my mouth shut and let skinny Orla do the talking. I'm not in Mrs. McEntee's good books.

"Yes, Miss, but it's Saturday, Miss," Orla said, as if butter wouldn't melt in her mouth.

Mrs. McEntee looked down her nose at us.

"There's gallons of blackberries out on the Gull Cliff," I said, quickly.

"Gallons, Miss," said Orla, picking up her cue.

We call Mrs. McEntee "Miss" although she is a "Mrs". We have never met Mr. McEntee. They live in a bungalow on the Portmannis Road just past the Field Centre, and he works in the No-Job Centre in Portmannis. Really it is called the Job Centre, but the No-Job Centre is what Brendan Egg calls it, and he is right. Mr. McEntee is not mad enough to go swimming in winter, and he never comes to our school so we never see him.

"Bramble jelly!" said Mrs. McEntee. "See you bring me a jar of your mother's best, Orla!"

She let us go. My plan had worked. If she had been meaning to stop us she had forgotten about it, thinking about the bramble jelly. I noticed she didn't ask me for any jelly. I haven't been getting on well with Mrs. McEntee over the past year. I mucked up her Ballyhannis Project. I didn't mean to do it. Damien Hughes and Colum Rice were teasing me and I chucked Owen Leary at Damien and missed and knocked the mast off Mrs. McEntee's Spanish Galleon. The Owen Leary I chucked wasn't the *real* one who killed the Spaniards; he was made of pipe cleaners and clay. I told Mrs. McEntee that it was supposed to be a wrecked Spanish Galleon and I couldn't see what harm wrecking it a bit more did. I think she had a word with Stella about it, because Stella gave me a speech about trying to behave better. She said I'd been through a difficult time, but people couldn't be expected to make allowances for me for ever.

We started across the causeway, banging our buckets and mucking about in the wet bits with our boots, trying to look as if we were just out for a walk, in case we were being watched by Gobber spies. Orla was very impressed by Brendan and his World War II Act, but I wasn't. I was beginning to wish I had stayed at home. I didn't fancy being caught between Brendan and a pack of kids from Belfast.

We didn't see a single Gobber!

By the time we reached the island Brendan and Damien should have been setting out but we couldn't see any sign of them. So much for Brendan and his *"Synchronise your watches"*. We were using Orla's old watch anyway, and it doesn't work well. Mine is bust, so I never know what time it is.

"Blackberrying first, or spying?" Orla asked, when we were safely among the rocks.

She had a look on her face that usually means trouble.

"What do you mean, *spying*?" I asked.

"To see what they're doing."

"You have been watching too many films on television," I said, firmly. "Blackberrying is what we came here to do, and that's what we will do."

Orla made a face, but she didn't argue about it. She flounced her red hair at me. I reckoned she'd been listening to Brendan too much.

Inishnagal isn't very big, but the going is hard. It took us about fifteen minutes from the time we came off the end of the causeway until we got up on to the sheep ground leading up to the Spaniards' House.

"It's very dark," Orla said.

"Now who's afraid?" I said.

"Shut up," she said.

We could see the glimmer of orange light from the lamppost at Egg's Corner, but not much else. We had decided not to bring torches, in case the flashes gave us away. We were relying on the moon, and there was a clear sky so that was all right. Otherwise the blackberries might have been difficult to find!

What we hadn't expected was the stillness around us. Maybe it was the weird shapes of old crumbling rocks around the Gull Cliff. I don't know. Stella says that Inishnagal is an island that wants to be left on its own, and that it would row out into the ocean if it could. I certainly felt that we weren't wanted there, but there was no way I could put it into words without sounding silly, or scared.

19

Brendan and Damien took their time about arriving.

"Old Miss was on the beach," Damien said, by way of explanation, and Brendan tried to look as if it was nothing to do with him. Brendan is still scared of Mrs. McEntee, even though he left our school years ago. He isn't the only one!

The two boys started work inside the Spaniards' House and I went up to the ruined gable end with Orla. I was glad that I had my wellingtons on, for I had to push right in to get at the blackberries, which were difficult enough to see anyway. I had a big thick jersey on, which I pulled right down over my wrists to stop them getting scratched. I had to take off my anorak because I had ripped my last one hunting bottles, and Stella would have killed me and told me my father wasn't made of anorak money if the brambles had ripped the new one.

Blackberrying is hard work but it isn't too bad, because you can eat a few as you go along. I am better at it than Orla, because she eats too many. She kept stopping to eat them, and then she went climbing up on the rocks and looked over. The Gull Cliff is very dangerous, all overhangs and soft shale. I was afraid the rock she was on would give way and she'd go tumbling down and break her neck.

"Don't fall!" I warned her.

"I'm all right," she said, and then the next

minute she came slithering off the rock with a giggle, and disappeared round the end of the Spaniards' House.

"Where are you going?" I called.

"Where's Orla gone?" Damien said, popping his head up from the bushes inside the house. He was down by the fallen window arch, trying to get the high ones. The best blackberries are in the house, which is why the boys had picked the inside for themselves.

"Is Orla mitching off?" Brendan said, sounding annoyed.

"Never you mind," I answered.

"I do mind, though," Brendan said.

"I expect she's spying on the Gobbers," I said.

"She'd be good at sneaking about," Damien said.

"Orla's not a sneak."

"She should have told me where she was going!" Brendan said, making out that he was our leader.

"Big Egg!" I said, scornfully.

He went mad! He nearly threw his bucket at me.

"You dry up, Nora-No-Guts!" he said. It was all because Damien was there. Big Egg was just a joke. I didn't mean to make him mad. But he got mad because I was calling him names in front of Damien.

21

"Who're you calling names?" I said, because I wasn't going to back down.

"You!" they both said. Damien would make you sick the way he agrees with everything Brendan says and eggs him on. Eggs. That's another of my Egg jokes, like Big Egg.

"Well, you shouldn't call me names," I said.

"Nora-Nora-No-Mum!" Damien sang out, suddenly.

Even Brendan looked shocked.

I don't like people calling me things like that. I could feel myself going trembly inside.

"Nora-No-Mum's going to cry!" Damien said.

"Leave her," Brendan said. I think he was a bit worried about the No-Mum bit, in case I told on them.

"Leave her here where the ghosties will get her!" Damien said. "Old Nora will run away home, won't you Nora?"

I didn't say a word.

"Come on, Damien," Brendan said, and he made Damien go off with him. Brendan knew how I felt about my mother and he would never have called me "No-Mum". I watched them go, hoping the Gobbers would catch Damien and clobber him.

It was very dark.

Orla should have come back. Supposing the Gobbers had caught her?

I didn't want to go on and leave her, but I

wasn't keen on staying either. I had to stay for a bit, though, or Damien would have the laugh on me. He would probably wait to see how long I stayed and if I left soon, he would say I was scared of dead Spaniards.

I had to stay.

Never mind if the Gobbers had caught Orla. They might be strangers, but they were just school kids. They weren't going to massacre her like Owen Leary and the Spaniards. They had their teacher with them, and if Orla turned up at their camp site she would probably be shown their weather gauges and be given a cup of tea and burnt sausages from their barbecue.

I had my bucket three-quarters full, and there was still no sign of Orla coming back.

Perhaps she had gone off home.

I thought I would change my position and go into the Spaniards' House to where the best berries were.

I worked my way in. I wasn't afraid, not a bit.

Brendan and Damien were afraid, and that was why they said I was afraid, so that they would have an excuse to slope off. Orla was afraid, too. She had probably gone home.

I was the only one not afraid to stay at the Spaniards' House in the dark, and I was going to make sure they all knew it. That would Nora-No-Guts them all right.

That was what I told myself, several times, but one part of me at least wasn't listening. All it wanted to do was to run home as fast as my legs would carry it!

Then I realised that I had stopped looking for blackberries, I was listening instead. Something had disturbed the gulls. I could hear them and I could hear another sound as well.

I was standing still with my hands clenched on the wire handle of my bucket, listening to something awful that I had never in my whole life thought I would hear.

It was a Sighing sound. It was a horrible, sing-song sound. It was in the house, all around me, welling out of the broken walls, and my feeling was that it was shoving at me, trying to push me out and away. It wanted me to go, but the terrible thing was that I hadn't the power to move. I was stuck with the sound of the Sighing all around me. The most I could manage was a shiver.

That shiver did it.

I ran and I ran and I ran and I ran away from that old ruin and I never looked back, not once.

Three

I didn't stop running until I came scrambling down on to the causeway, scratched and bruised from taking the direct route over the rocks and briars with no heed for anything but to get off the island as quickly as I could.

My heart was thumping like a drum!

I'd heard the Sighing. Every place has its own ghost story, and the Headland is no different. The Spaniards that Owen Leary massacred were our bogey men, and the story of the Sighing had given Inishnagal its reputation. I'd scared the wits out of our Chris with it not long after the wits had been scared out of me the self same way. Like all bogey men stories, nobody really believed it, but now, crossing the causeway with the moonlight glistening on the water at Slaughter Point I believed it sure enough! I believed it, but who would believe me?

I was scared stiff!

I will not be afraid, I told myself. *It was only imagination.*

I made a poor job of convincing myself, but I made myself slow down just the same, to prove it.

I came off the end of the causeway, and spotted somebody at the door of Egg's Shop, picked out by the orange light at the corner.

It was our Stella, being an ambush for Nora-out-too-late.

What could I do? I *could* go the long way, up the cliff path and down the lane to our house, but that meant walking along the beach in the darkness towards Slaughter Point and I wasn't in the mood for that! The alternative was to go down towards Egg's Corner in the shadow of the wall. Then I could slip into Egg's shop and hide there till Stella went away, none the wiser. When she went, I could nip across the lane and into Cully's field on the other side of the wall, which would give me an even chance of beatling up the hill and in through our back window while Stella was walking up the lane. Then I could be half way into my pyjamas with the kettle on the range for a cup of tea and I-was-wondering-where-you'd-got-to-at-this-time-of-night-Stella, with never a thought in my mind that she might have been on a Nora hunt.

It would have been different if she had been my mother. My mother would have bought me something in Egg's shop and walked me up home, but Stella is always jumpy about me.

I got into Egg's shop, according to plan. I settled down amongst our bottles, which was as good a hiding place as any. We bring bottles into

Mrs. Egg and she gives us four pence a bottle instead of the five pence the people who throw them away would get. Stella says she is mean but I don't see why Mrs. Egg shouldn't have her penny a bottle profit.

I could hear them talking, through the back door of the shop. I wouldn't have listened, but I heard Stella mention my name. If my name was mentioned it was my business, so I was all right to listen!

"A pair of bright sparks," Mrs. Egg said. I think she meant me and Orla.

"Too bright for their own business," Stella said, grumpily.

I wasn't pleased. I didn't think Stella should be discussing me like that.

"Nora's not what she was," said Mrs. Egg. "Och, the poor things! Herself and Chris . . . it's hard on the children."

Stella didn't say anything.

"They're missing their mother," Mrs. Egg said. "It's only to be expected. Nobody can take the place of a child's own mother."

"Nobody would expect to," said Stella, stiffly.

"Children know all sorts of things you'd never credit them with," said Mrs. Egg.

I didn't know what she meant, but I did know that she didn't mean it to be taken kindly. Mrs. Egg is that sort of person. She has a voice she puts on when she wants to get at you. She sounds

27

extra kind and careful and concerned, but really she is waiting to see if she can rile you. That was what she was doing to Stella.

"I hear you had trouble this morning with the Belfast children," Stella said, changing the subject.

"We'd be better off without them!" Mrs. Egg said.

"I hope Nora and Chris were not involved," Stella said.

As if I wasn't in trouble enough! I held my breath, wondering what Mrs. Egg would say. Who had been telling Stella about the fight in the lane? In a moment Mrs. Egg would open her mouth and I'd be burnt at the stake, or worse.

"Young Chris wouldn't hurt a fly," Mrs. Egg said, carefully not mentioning me. "I don't know what those people think they're doing, bringing the sweepings of the city streets down here."

Stella didn't say anything for a moment. I could just imagine her face. Stella is from Belfast herself.

"I wouldn't call them that," she said. "The children in the city have had a hard time. You can't expect little sweetie-pies."

"Strangers are all right, if they don't interfere with you," Mrs. Egg said.

That was one in the eye for Stella! Stella may be the smartest brain in Ballyhannis bar me, but there are lots of things she does not know, and one of them is how to sort with a person like Mrs. Egg. Mrs. Egg has been around a long time, and there have been Eggs in Ballyhannis ever since anybody can remember. I know Mrs. Egg doesn't take kindly to strangers saying what Ballyhannis people should and should not be doing. When she said, "Strangers are all right if they don't interfere with you," Mrs. Egg was by-the-way talking about the Gobbers, but really she was having a side kick at Stella herself.

"Yes," said Stella.

There was a long, uncomfortable pause.

"Is there anything else I can get you, dear?" Mrs. Egg said, and I heard the till rattle. From the rattle of it I could tell that she had started counting the coins to show Stella that it was time to close, and Stella had outstayed her welcome.

"Chase Nora up the hill if you see her," said Stella.

"She's a quiet wee thing, nearly as quiet as young Chris," Mrs. Egg said. "She'll not need chasing."

The way she said it made it sound as though Stella was some sort of bully.

A quiet wee thing. I didn't like that! Nora-No-Guts again!

I heard Stella going out of the shop, which was

my cue to get my skates on if I was to make it up to our house without getting caught.

I nipped out of the back store, up the path, and dodged across the area where the light from Egg's lamppost falls, and hopped over the wall into Cully's field, where I scared the daylights out of his bullock!

It was no great problem to beat Stella up the lane to our house, though I had to move doubled up through the fields, in case she spotted me.

The only trouble I got into was when I reached our back window and found that Stella had snibbed it. She does not like us coming through the back window – she likes Orla coming through it even less – and when she remembers she puts the snib on, but I was prepared for that. I had my pen-knife in my anorak pocket, and all I had to do was to put the thin blade between the sashes of the window and push it along, so that the window snib was pushed back.

That was when I pulled up with a start.

My pen-knife was in my anorak, and my anorak was still at the Spaniards' House, draped over a bush where I'd left it. That meant going back for it, but with Stella on the rampage there was no time for that.

I raced round to the front of the house as quickly as I could, and in through the door. So long as Stella hadn't seen me without the anorak she couldn't ask me to go back for it. One place I *wasn't* going was back to the island!

Chris was sitting on the sofa, with Erk and Leary all over him.

"You're late," Chris said, brushing his hair out of his eyes. He was in his dressing-gown. Leary stretched out lazily, trying to look like a pet pussy instead of the dreaded Mouse Massacre-er of Ballyhannis. Chris tickled Leary's tummy. "Stella is out for your blood," he said.

"I know," I said. "You tell her I was in here the minute after she went out, and she must have missed me in the dark."

"I'll tell her no such thing," Chris said, indignantly. He may be small and quiet and talk mostly to animals, but when he decides to stick up for himself he can be fierce enough. "You do your own lying."

"I'm no liar," I said.

"You are when it suits you," he said.

"You're not going to tell Stella I've just come in this minute, are you?" I said.

"Why not, if it is true?"

"Because it would be a dirty, rotten, sneaky thing to do," I said, bitterly.

"Okay," Chris said. "I'll get off side, where I won't be asked, and won't have to tell any lies."

He went off to his room clutching Leary. Erk padded after him.

I stuck the kettle on the range and settled

down on the sofa with *Radio Times* as though I'd been in for ages and was just wondering if there would be anything good on T.V. We have a portable T.V. that Stella brought with her from her digs in Belfast, when she came. It is black and white and not as good as the Donnellys' colour one, but it is better than nothing at all, which is what we had before Stella came. When Stella isn't looking I sometimes take it upstairs to bed with me. I like watching T.V. in bed, and she doesn't notice till too late when she is working at her books.

Stella came in.

"Oh, hullo," I said, trying to sound like a fairy off a Christmas Tree. "Shall I make you a cup of tea?"

"Yes," she said, and she slumped down in the big chair. She is quite pretty, Stella. She has dark eyes and reddy-brown hair and she wears green eye-shadow that Mrs. Egg doesn't like. I heard Mrs. Egg telling Mrs. McEntee about it.

"Did you hear anything interesting about yourself, hiding round the back in Egg's shop?" Stella asked, suddenly.

I was so surprised that I didn't know what to say! How was I to know that she had seen me? Seen me? She *couldn't* have seen me! The door of the back store was half across, and she couldn't have seen through it unless her eye-shadow was special X-Ray stuff, which it wasn't.

I opened my mouth to say something, and shut it again. I must have looked daft, sitting there opening and shutting it.

"Clinking bottles!" Stella said.

"Oh," I said.

"Well, did you hear well of yourself?"

"I couldn't help hearing," I said, defensively. "I wasn't in there to overhear. I was just . . ." There I faded out again, because I didn't want to admit that I was hiding from her.

"You're so sharp that you'll cut yourself, one of these days," Stella said.

"I didn't mean any harm."

"You hurt yourself, not me, Nora," she said. "If you want to turn into a deceitful and dishonest person, now is the time to get in some early practice."

"I'm sorry."

"So you should be!"

"I didn't mean to overhear."

Stella gave me a hard look. Just at that moment I didn't like Stella very much. She had no call to say I was deceitful and dishonest when all I had done was to accidentally overhear her conversation. *Almost* accidentally.

"I'm not going to ask you what you've been doing till this time of night, Nora," Stella said.

"I was out," I said.

"I know you were out. I know where you were, too!" she said, and she fished in the pocket of her coat and tossed my envelope, the one with TO BE OPENED IF WE DO NOT RETURN printed across it, on to the sofa. "I read your note. That was bad enough."

"It was the truth!" I said.

"If you had told me properly, I would not have let you go," she said.

"Why not? I'm big enough to go over to the island on my own. And anyway I wasn't on my own. I was with Orla and Brendan and Damien."

"No more going to the island after dark," Stella said. "Your father would have a fit! I've heard enough stories about that place. Deep water and currents and those crumbling rocks at the Gull Cliff."

"You know nothing about it!" I said. "Anyway, Daddy wouldn't mind," I added.

We were standing facing each other by this time. Tears pricked at my eyelids.

"The four of you were going over to make trouble for those Belfast children," Stella said. "That was what it was all about, wasn't it? Brendan and Damien up to their tricks, with you two backing them up."

"We went for blackberries!" I said.

"Where are they then?"

I knew where my blackberries were. They were in my bucket. But where was my bucket?

"I must have left them in Egg's shop," I said.

"I'll believe you, thousands wouldn't!" Stella said, in a totally disbelieving voice.

It was true, and she wouldn't believe me!

"You don't *want* to believe me! You don't like me. I don't know why you stay here. You don't like anything I do!" I was stamping mad and fed up with being called a liar and got at for listening to other people's conversations and accused of acting like Brendan and Damien and carrying on like some sort of juvenile delinquent, when all the time I knew I wasn't like that at all.

"I wish my Daddy was back here, and you would go away!" I said, and I got out of the room and beat it up the stairs to my own room, where I put the bolt on and wouldn't come out, even if Stella came up to drag me out. I put the chair against the inside of the door as well.

Stella didn't come upstairs after me.

She left me alone to think about it.

Four

The next morning I didn't say a word to anybody. I just cleared off to the shore after church, with Erk for company.

Chris thinks he owns Erk, but he doesn't. Erk was in our family before Chris was born. I own Erk as much as he does.

I was down on the shore skimming stones for Erk to bark at when Orla came after me. Erk doesn't chase stones any more, he knows they sink.

"Nora-Nora-Nora," Orla started off, in her usual way.

"Shut up," I said, not very politely, but I wasn't feeling polite.

"What's the matter with you?" she said, her face falling.

"I'm fed up," I said. "I'm fed up with Mrs. McEntee being cross with me at school and Stella blasting off at me at home, and *you!*"

"What are you fed up with me for?" Orla asked. Her face was puffy because of whatever was wrong with her teeth.

"You went sneaking off home and left me all alone on the island," I said.

"I didn't! Brendan and Damien were with you!"

"They got scared and went away, I was left waiting for you, and you just went off home or something and then when I got home I was late and Stella grabbed me. It's all your fault!" I finished up, although I knew it wasn't. I wanted somebody to be fed up at, apart from myself. Orla was supposed to be my friend, and she should have been helping me, not leaving me in the lurch, especially when the whole idea of crossing over to the island at night to pick blackberries was hers to begin with.

"Oh!" Orla said.

I chucked another stone for Erk.

"I went round by the pier, looking for Gobbers," Orla said. "I was spying!"

"Big deal!"

"I couldn't be bothered coming back, so I went home."

"Thanks a lot," I said.

"I don't know what you are so fussed about," Orla said.

I wasn't going to tell her about the Sighing, because it would make me look silly, and she would tell everyone. What could I have told her anyway? It would sound as if I'd got frightened of my own shadow at the Spaniards' House. No good trying to explain that it wasn't the dark and the loneliness that frightened me.

Erk barked at me. I'd forgotten about his stones.

"Nora?" Orla said. I picked up another stone for Erk. It did eight jumps, which is nothing like my best, but the sea was choppy.

"Just because you hadn't the sense to come home," she said. "Brendan and Damien got home all right, didn't they? I got home. What did you get up to out there that kept you?"

"Nothing."

"Then what's the matter?"

"Nothing. Not-a-thing."

"I'll tell you what I came to tell you then," Orla said, in a determined to be friendly voice.

I'd forgotten about her Nora-Nora-Nora-ing.

"Tell me."

"Damien and Colum Rice have got one of the Gobbers in a Gobber Trap, down by the harbour. Damien says they are going to pay him back for stoning us and getting me wet."

"How did he find out about that?"

She'd told him. Well, maybe she hadn't. Ballyhannis is a small place.

"They're going to punch his face in when they get him," Orla said, sounding excited.

"I thought you said they'd trapped him already."

"Got him cornered," said Orla. "They're not a

38

bit soft. They chased him down the beach, and now he's Gobber Trapped, because he's down by the harbour and he'll have to go past them to get back to the island. Damien says he is going to teach the Gobber to leave Ballyhannis people alone."

"Serve the Gobber right," I said, uneasily.

"Are you coming to see?"

I chucked another stone.

"Come on," Orla said.

I didn't much want to go, but on the other hand I didn't want to fall out with Orla. In the back of my mind was the thought that sooner or later – *sooner* rather than later – I was going to have to go back to the island to get my anorak, and I didn't like the idea of going back on my own, even in broad daylight. If I wanted company, Orla was my best bet.

"All right," I said.

We walked along by the tide with Erk lolloping beside us, wagging his tail. I caught sight of Colum's red jersey near the harbour. He was hiding down behind the rocks with a stick in his hands, and he gave us a shush sign and pointed. Damien was creeping along by the old sluice-pipe with a stick of his own, which was the haft of an old spade.

"Hunt the Gobber!" I said. I didn't like the look of Damien's weapon. Damien is always trying to prove that he is as tough as Brendan.

"Hold on to Erk," Orla said, so I took Erk by the collar.

Damien and Colum aren't very sensible, and it looked as if there was going to be a bad fight. If there was a fight I didn't want to be part of it, because Stella might get mad if I was.

But like it or not, Orla and I were both mixed up in it. We had been ever since Orla chucked part of my apple at the Gobbers, which gave Damien and Colum the chance to be big heroes at our expense. The only good thing was that Brendan wasn't with them. Brendan never knows when to stop when Damien is with him. He broke James Ogle's arm once.

"Do you think we should stop them?" I asked.

"Why?" Orla said.

Colum had worked his way round the side of the harbour. All at once he shouted and made a dive down off the rocks and on to the harbour wall, disappearing over it in pursuit of somebody we couldn't see.

Erk didn't like it. He started tugging to get away from me. Damien came running along the top of the sluice-pipe waving his spade haft and yahooing like mad.

"Come on!" Orla said, and we started across the sand, heading for the harbour wall. We got there and climbed up on it. By that time Damien and Colum were right down in the harbour itself, on the sand, and they had the Gobber by both arms.

They held an arm each, and Damien was twisting so that the Gobber's face was down in the sludgy black sand of the harbour bottom.

"Eat dirt!" Damien said, twisting hard.

The Gobber gave a yell. It was the skin head one, and he sounded as if Damien was really hurting him.

"Eat it!" Colum said, triumphantly. He twisted hard at his side, and the Gobber's face went down into the muck again.

Damien pressed his knee hard into the Gobber's back, pushing the Gobber's chest down.

"Gobble it all up!" he shouted.

The Gobber was crying and I was afraid that somebody was going to get badly hurt, probably the Gobber. Suddenly whether he was a Gobber or not didn't seem to matter very much.

"Stop it!" I shouted.

Orla looked at me. Then she said, "Yes, you stop it. You're just a pair of bullies." She didn't sound as if she meant it.

Damien grinned, and gave the Gobber another bash in the back.

"Nice dirt, isn't it?" Colum said.

"You stop it, Colum Rice!" I said, getting really worked up.

"Oh, and who is going to stop us?" Damien

said, and he eased his grip. At that moment the
Gobber gave a wriggle and hooked Damien's
ankle. Damien went off balance, and the Gobber
kicked his knee and Damien went over into the
dirty muck of the harbour bed, right on the seat
of his pants. It served him right.

Colum swung his stick to hit the Gobber and
the Gobber grabbed at him, and the next minute
the Gobber did something extraordinary.

The Gobber bit Colum's leg, hard!

Colum gave a howl and tried to kick the
Gobber, but the Gobber got clear. Colum sat
down holding his leg and howling blue murder.

"Right!" Damien said, in a horrid voice.
He picked up his spade haft and came forward,
wagging it. He was going to belt the Gobber with
it.

The Gobber had something in his hands. It
was a bit of old tie chain, slimey from lying in the
muck and dirt of the harbour bottom. It was a
frightening looking weapon, and the Gobber was
sobbing and swinging it, all at the same time.

"Lay off him, Damien," I said. "Somebody'll
get hurt."

Damien never even looked at me.

"Lay off him, or I'll tell."

Erk started growling. He could see I was mad.

"I'll loose the dog on you."

"I'll *kill* the dog!" Damien said.

"I'll let him go," I said.

Erk was nearly tugging my arm off. His teeth were bared, and the hair on his back was bristly. He was much stronger than I thought he was. I felt a bit afraid of him, and tightened my grip on his collar.

Colum sat where he was. There were tears in his eyes. The Gobber had really hurt him.

"Let Erk go, Nora!" Orla said. She was white in the face. "Let Erk go."

Erk snarled at the three of them.

"I'll tell on you, Damien Hughes," I said. "You've no call to go real fighting to hurt like that, two on one."

"I'll see to you later, Nora-No-Guts," Damien said, but he was moving sideways now. Erk had really impressed him. He was afraid of Erk's teeth. So was I! I've never seen old Erk turn on anybody like that.

The Gobber was standing against the harbour wall, holding the filthy length of chain. He was muck to the eyebrows, and crying in a heaving, sobbing way, but from the way he was holding the chain it was clear he wasn't going to let any of us go near him without getting hurt.

"Come on, Colum," Damien said. "Let's see your leg." He helped Colum up. "We'll get you for this," Damien said to the Gobber.

Erk growled and tugged my arm half off to get at them.

"Stop it, Erk," I said, but inside I was proud of him.

"You and your dog too, Nora-No-Guts," Damien said.

They went off over the rocks, with Colum sniffing and complaining, and Damien helping him along.

The Gobber was still holding the chain, looking as if he wanted to kill somebody with it.

"You keep that dog off me!" she said.

We could tell the Gobber was a girl, once we'd heard her speak. She didn't look like a girl, because she was so busy being a skin head. She was all plastered with mud and in a terrible mess, her face puffed with crying.

Orla moved toward her, and the girl swung the chain. Erk snarled, and pulled forward. She swung at him and missed.

"You get away from me," she said. "You and your dirty old dog!"

"Don't you hit my dog!"

"I'll finish you if you come near me," she said.

"Go on!" I said. "Who needs you here? Away home."

"I've as much right here as you have," she said.

"You have not," said Orla. "This is our place."

The Gobber girl went off, steering a wide course round Erk. I had to keep a firm grip on him or he'd have had the pants off her. Erk doesn't like people who have a go at me.

"We should have helped her clean herself up," I said to Orla.

"Why?"

"She might have been hurt. They were really laying into her."

"They thought she was a boy," Orla said. "She looks like a boy."

"Doesn't make any difference. They had no right to lay into her."

We walked back toward Egg's Corner.

The Gobber girl had gone down on to the shore, where she was bathing her face in the sea. She looked up as we went past, but she didn't wave or anything.

She gave us a 'V' sign.

"You see?" Orla said. "That's all the thanks you get!"

"My anorak's on the island," I said.

We both thought about it. We were sitting on the wall outside Egg's Shop. The Gobber girl had already gone back across the causeway, and she would be full of tales about what the Ballyhannis people had done to her.

"It'll have to stay there," Orla said. "You can't risk going for it. Not after this."

"Damien's a wee thug!" I said.

"She hurt Colum."

"Erk was great!"

Old Erk was wagging his tail at me, making out how brave he'd been, but I bet he was scared. It was scary. It wasn't the kind of fighting I'm used to, where people punch each other. Colum and Damien had intended to hurt the Gobber, and she meant to hurt them with her teeth, and the chain.

"They're very tough, those Gobbers," Orla said. "And some of them are big."

"Very big," I said.

"We started it, I suppose," said Orla.

"*You* started it, you mean."

"But that was only kid's stuff, with the apple," Orla said.

The trouble was that Damien and Colum were kids, trying not to be. They wanted to be as big as Brendan Egg. Brendan was a sad case, hanging round the place with nothing to do. The only people he could impress were people like Damien and Colum. He was a big soft baby kid himself for bothering about what they thought, but I couldn't help feeling sorry for him. He used to fix my bike for me, when I had a bike, and he was always slipping Erk things out of the shop. His mother doesn't let him near the shop now, since he started taking cigarettes.

Those big Gobbers were probably like Brendan, trying to make themselves look

important, when really they had nothing to be
important about.

"Brendan will be getting mixed up in it next,"
I said. "You wait and see!"

Five

The next morning, which was Monday morning, something happened almost at once.

We were in school at first lesson when there was a knock at the door and in came the Gobbers' teacher and the Gobber girl.

I looked at Orla.

Damien and Colum were together at the back of the classroom. When we turned round to look at them they had both gone green.

The teacher talked to Mrs. McEntee. Mrs. McEntee went very funny, like setting concrete. She had gone damp grey. It was interesting. I have never seen anybody change colour like that before.

She talked to the Gobber girl, who was looking very scared. The Gobber girl didn't say much.

Whatever was said, we couldn't hear any of it, because we were busy trying not to be noticed. We have to sit at the front so that Mrs. McEntee can keep an eye on us, and it wasn't very easy trying to be invisible.

If the teacher had come to report Damien and Colum he might report me and Orla too. I could imagine Stella believing me when I tried to explain that old Erk had saved the Gobber girl from getting a beating. She would think we had been part of it. The Gobber girl probably thought we were anyway.

"Everybody put down their books, please," Mrs. McEntee said.

We put down our books. Orla sat with her head down, but I didn't think that that would do any good.

If we were going to be caught, it would be awful. We might be sent to prison or one of those schools where they march you about and shout at you. Cormac Hughes got sent to one of those for stealing.

"I've just been told a terrible thing," said Mrs. McEntee. "A thing I hoped I'd never hear, which seems to be about some pupils from this school."

She paused and let the worry hang over our heads. I didn't dare look at Orla. I just looked straight ahead. I'd gone all dried up inside.

Dear-God-don't-let-it-happen. Dear-God-don't-let-it-happen. Dear-God-don't-let-it-happen. I kept repeating inside myself.

"Mr. Brennan tells me that a child from his party has been badly beaten up by a gang of children down by our harbour." She tapped her fingers on her desk. "Mr. Brennan thinks it must have been children from this school who were responsible. Has anybody anything to say?"

I looked at Orla. She looked as if she might start crying any minute.

If we didn't say anything, we were as good as admitting that we had been part and parcel of it. What had happened wasn't our fault, and we'd tried to stop it once we'd realised how serious it was getting, but would anybody believe us? If we put our hands up and told on Colum and Damien we would have them after us whatever Mrs. McEntee said, because she couldn't be watching them all the time. We couldn't win either way.

I was well and truly frightened out of my little pink skin, and I wasn't the only one. You could have heard a pin drop in our class.

"Nobody feels like owning up, I see," said Mrs. McEntee, grimly, and our chance of owning up was gone. "Right! I want all fourteen Senior children out here, in a row, where we can get a good look at you."

Mr. Brennan said something, as though he didn't think it was a good idea, but Mrs. McEntee gave him one of her looks and went ahead with what she was doing. It was her school and he was just a stranger there.

We all trooped out. It was like an identity

parade in a detective film, only worse, because it was real, and it was happening to us, and Orla and I were the ones likely to be picked out. Damien and Colum would be picked out too, but then they'd done something. They deserved it. Maybe we did too. We hadn't started stopping the fight until it was almost too late.

"Now, dear," said Mrs. McEntee to the Gobber girl. "Do you recognise any of the children here?"

The Gobber girl looked really miserable. She was a scrawny looking thing to begin with, with her skin head haircut and little wire earring, but now she looked much worse because the side of her face was puffy and swollen as a result of the fight. I concentrated on her earring and not on horrible skinny her and her denim jacket.

She looked at us, and we looked at her. I looked at her, anyway, willing her to say nothing. I don't know what Orla and Colum and Damien did.

"Well?" Mrs. McEntee said.

The girl sucked her swollen lip and looked as if she might be going to cry, but she didn't say anything.

"Nobody's going to hurt you any more, dear," Mrs. McEntee prompted. "We only want to find out who was responsible and make sure that this sort of thing doesn't happen again."

"Do you see anybody, Crystal?" Mr. Brennan asked. I don't think he thought the identity parade was a good idea, from the way he said it.

"No, Sir," the Gobber girl said. She had her eyes down when she said it.

"Crystal?" said Mrs. McEntee.

"No, Miss," said Crystal.

I was never so relieved as when I got back to my seat and never so surprised either. I had us already arrested and locked up in jail or worse, with Stella and Mrs. McEntee and Mrs. Donnelly having hysterics all over the place and nobody believing that Orla and I had tried to stop it.

Mrs. McEntee and Crystal and Mr. Brennan went out of the room.

Orla puffed out her cheeks at me.

"I thought we were goners for sure," I said.

Mrs. McEntee came back into the room.

"Well?" she said, closing the door behind her.

Everybody sat up and tried to look good. There had been a great chatter just before she came in, but it stopped in a flash.

"Well, has anybody anything to say?"

"Maybe it was somebody else, Miss," said Big Sally Colley.

"It was shameful, that's what it was!" said Mrs. McEntee. "I have my own ideas about who might have been involved, and I'll be keeping my eye on a few individuals, I can tell you."

"Miss, the Gobbers are awful tough," Marcus Toal said.

Then there was a bubble of talk, with people telling things about the Gobbers, and somebody mentioned Orla getting soaked.

"I don't want to hear another word!" said Mrs. McEntee. "Those children are visitors down here. They're here to learn about nature, and the only lesson they're getting is human nature! One defenceless girl hopped on by a gang."

"She's a Gobber, Miss," said James Rice.

"Gobbers aren't defenceless, Miss," said Colum.

"They're all the same. They came down here looking for fights!"

"That girl wasn't looking for a fight. She was walking along the beach!" said Mrs. McEntee. "You stick offensive labels on people, and then you decide you can attack them. I'm ashamed of the whole un-Christian pack of you."

Her face had gone from cement grey to reddy cream.

Nobody said a word.

"Now you will get out your books again and get on with your work, and heaven help the child who crosses me this day!" she said.

"She'd no call to call us un-Christian!" Sally Colley said. Big Sally is very Holy Mary and down to Mass in Portmannis every morning before she comes to school. It is a long way to go to Mass but they go in her father's car and never mind the petrol. Her sister Nuala went to the Nun's School in Portmannis but Mrs. Colley had a row with Sister Bernadette when Nuala didn't get her exam, and now we are stuck with Sally. I bet Sister Bernadette was well pleased to see the back of her.

"It is a mystery," Roisin Smith said, all goggle eyed. "The Mystery of Who Beat Up The Gobber." Roisin is an E. Blyton maniac. She has the life pestered out of the lady on the library bus with request cards. Everybody else could make a good guess at Who Beat Up The Gobber without having to make a mystery of it.

I went looking for Damien and Colum, but they had made themselves scarce.

"Hiding!" I told Orla.

We knew their usual hiding places, the bins at the bike shed and behind the coats in the coat rooms, but they weren't in either.

"Toilets!" Orla said.

The Boys is an old brick shed with a tin roof at the side of the school, and sure enough the door was bolted shut and wouldn't open when we kicked it. We tried pinging stones at the roof but they wouldn't come out until the bell went, and when they did appear it was too late to do anything. The only word we got was a note from Damien, handed forward down the desks:

"YOU'RE FOR IT IF YOU TELL"

"Big Deal", Orla whispered, and Mrs. McEntee looked up. Orla scrunched up the note and popped it into her mouth to hide it. Even though it was a small note, it was a stupid thing to do. I forgot to ask her if she swallowed it.

We walked up the lane together after school. Stella had a cup of tea for us, and some of her toast and homemade jam. I think she was trying to make up to me.

"I like your Stella," Orla said, when she was leaving.

"Umh!" I said. I wasn't sure about Stella, just then. I was half afraid of her, for a start. I was afraid she might go away, and then my father would be mad. She wasn't really in our family, she could just go if she decided to, and she might decide to if she took against me. It wasn't like having my mother there, the way it used to be. Stella was just putting in time. My mother knew everybody and got on with everybody and didn't try to tell people what they should be doing, like Stella. My mother was great friends with people like Mrs. Egg. Maybe that was another reason why Mrs. Egg didn't take to Stella.

When I got back into the house after leaving Orla up the field by her house, Stella had disappeared to her desk upstairs and her books, and I had the downstairs to myself and Erk.

I sat down on the window ledge. I could see Inishnagal. I couldn't see any Gobbers, but that wasn't surprising because Orla said they had pitched their tents at the little pier, down by the far end. It isn't really a pier at all. Some daft people tried to live there once, and made the pier, but one winter finished them.

Chris came in.

"Hey!" I said. "How are you?"

He never said a word, not even to Erk though the big dog lolloped over to him. Old Erk is getting slow, even if he still knows how to be fierce.

Chris chucked down his bag and ran upstairs to his room.

"Chris? Was that Chris?" Stella called.

"Somebody just like him," I said. "Maybe it was his doppelganger!" A doppelganger is a sort of double. Orla told me about them. They are very scary. Then I thought maybe Stella thought I was being cheeky. If she did, I was sorry, but I couldn't take it back, could I?

"Would you ask him if he wants some toast, Nora?" Stella said, sticking her head over the bannisters. She was up there, she could have asked him easily, but I suppose she wanted to get on with her books.

"Who is going to make it?" I said.

"You can make it, I'm busy," Stella said.

For a moment I was mad! I could have told her that I had had a busy day too, being identity paraded and in danger of spending the rest of my days in Borstal or prison or wherever they put people who beat people up.

I buttoned down the feeling. She *was* busy. I climbed the stairs and knocked on Chris's door, but he didn't answer.

"Chris? Do you want some toast? Stella says I'm to make you some!" I said the bit about Stella extra loudly, so that she would hear me. He didn't answer.

"Doesn't want any," I reported to Stella, poking my head round her door.

"Huh?" she said, not really paying any attention. She gets like that when she has her head in books. She calls it deep concentration and says she has to be like that to get her work right, but I don't know.

"Never mind," I said. I went downstairs and pinched some blackberries from my blackberry bucket, which she still hadn't got round to boiling up. After all the fuss, she'd barely said "Thank you" when I brought the bucket up from Egg's Shop, and there was no apology for disbelieving me. On the other hand when she is busy she often doesn't remember things like that, things that don't seem important to her but mean a lot to other people.

Chris came downstairs with Leary in his arms. Chris's face was all red and funny.

"You've been crying, Chris," I said. "What's happened?"

"Just mind your own business," he said, and he went out of the door with Leary giving me one of his Mouse-Massacre-er look over his shoulder.

I let him go. I had trouble enough of my own to be getting on with!

Six

We were all sure that the Gobbers would be out for revenge after what had happened to Crystal. We knew something would happen, but the big question was what?

Brendan, Damien and Colum and their friends had a meeting, and afterwards they went round giving orders.

"Keep in pairs and keep away from them," Brendan told everyone. "If you are attacked, yell for us, and we'll look after you."

"You're not looking after me," I said. "You just want to show off how tough you are."

"Okay," Brendan said. "You get your face shoved in by Gobbers. See if I care."

"You and Colum and Damien have caused all the trouble," I said.

"That's right," said Orla, sticking up for me.

"Is it?" said Brendan. "Who started it then?"

He meant who had the first fight with the Gobbers, and of course he was right. Orla had started it by chucking the apple, but then the boys went round making a thing about the Gobbers attacking us, and Damien and Colum had to show how smart they were by Gobber-Trapping Crystal. The next thing would be an army of Gobbers who were used to tough fighting in Belfast coming over to smash up Ballyhannis.

"Serve us right too," I said, glumly, thinking of what Mrs. McEntee had said. Right from the start we had all been ready for trouble from the Gobbers.

As luck would have it, it was Orla who got caught again.

She was down on the beach with Donnelly's buggy which is the bottom of Orla's pram with one of Egg's orange boxes on top. Brendan Egg made it for her; he didn't make it well and it isn't much good but she uses it to gather driftwood. She was pushing it down by the rocks when she found a whole pack of Gobbers had come over the causeway and surrounded her, reversing the Gobber Trap.

"Why didn't you run away?" I asked her later.

"It is our shore," she said. "I'm not running away from anybody on my own shore."

I think she was silly. I would have run away, or escaped by climbing up the cliff path beyond Slaughter Point. She couldn't have taken the buggy with her if she had used the cliff path and she says she wasn't going to let the Gobbers have her buggy. I'd rather have a bust buggy than a fractured face, but maybe Orla is braver than I am. Anyway, she stayed. She saw them coming, but she decided to pay no attention to them and hope for the best.

The next thing was that a big one came up to her and said, "We're looking for the two with the sticks."

He meant Damien and Colum. They didn't know about Brendan yet. He was our secret weapon.

Orla said nothing.

They wouldn't let her past.

Then the Gobber girl showed up, the skin head one.

"What about this one, Crystal?" the biggest boy asked her.

"She was there," Crystal said.

"What'll we do to her, Crystal?"

They all started making suggestions and Orla says she was beginning to get frightened.

"Cut off her hair."

"Smash up her truck."

"You want to fight her Crystal? We'll hold your coat."

Orla says the big boy who said this said it with a sort of sneer.

"She was trying to stop it, Aldo," Crystal said.

"Was she?" said Aldo, and he gave Orla's hair a tug which brought tears to her eyes. Orla says she would have been crying already only she was

61

so cross, and she didn't want to give them the satisfaction.

"That's one of the ones that set the dog on Crystal!"

That got them excited.

Orla thought it wouldn't do any good trying to explain that Erk was my dog. They wouldn't have believed her. Anyway, she says she wouldn't have done it. Orla *must* be braver than me. I would have done almost anything to get away.

"What's your name?" Aldo kept asking Orla, and in the end Orla told him.

"Where'd you get your funny hair?" Aldo said, and gave Orla's famous red hair a tug.

"Just you leave me alone!" Orla said, and they all started laughing, as if it was dead funny.

Orla was lucky, because at that moment she was saved.

Mr. Brennan came round the corner of Egg's Shop, and he saw what was happening at once. The Gobbers saw him coming, and they ran off. All except Crystal.

She stood looking at Orla. Crystal was peculiar looking. She had her hair cut close to her head the way skin heads do, and she had dirty looking denims with things written on them, and her eyebrows were all plucked. You'd never catch anybody in Ballyhannis dressing like that!

"You all right?" she asked Orla.

"No thanks to you," said Orla.

"I don't want you," said Crystal. "It's the one that tried to set the dog on me I want!"

You can tell I was pleased when Orla told me that. I hadn't set the dog on her. I'd used Erk to protect her, but she must have thought I was attacking her just because I wasn't a Gobber like her.

Mr. Brennan came running up.

"What's all this, Crystal?" he said. "Making friends?"

"Some hope Sir," Crystal said. Orla says he knew fine well they weren't making friends.

"What's been going on?" he asked, looking at the wrecked buggy, with the wood strewn around it. "We'd better give this young lady a hand to pick up her wood, Crystal," he said, when neither of them said anything. Crystal looked for a minute as if she was going to refuse, and then she did what he asked her. Orla says she only *just* did it, dropping a piece or two into the buggy, and then mooching around. Mr. Brennan gave her a hard look.

"I thought I told you to stay on the island, Crystal?" he said. "We don't want you in any more trouble."

"Aldo made me come, Sir," Crystal said.

"I'll have to sort that out with Aldo," Mr. Brennan said. Orla says she was pleased that Aldo had it coming, and she had a notion that Crystal was too. Crystal was the only skin head Gobber we saw, and Orla says she thinks the others got at her for being one.

"Can I go now, Sir?" Crystal asked, when the buggy was re-loaded.

"What about your friend here?"

"She's not my friend!"

"I'm not her friend!"

The two of them spoke at once.

Mr. Brennan shrugged, but he didn't say anything. He walked over and started reading some of the things the Gobbers had written on the sand:

GOBBER RULE OK!

GOBBER GUN RULE

"I see we've brought Belfast with us, Crystal," he said.

Crystal said nothing. She just scratched her pointy nose.

Orla hooked up her buggy and began to drag it along the shore. By this time she says she had calmed down a bit, but she was still churned up inside, and a bit frightened.

She was certainly looking frightened when I met her pushing the buggy up the lane. She told me all about what had happened to her, including the bit about Crystal being out to get me for setting my dog on her, and then she said: "I wish Brendan had been there."

"Oh, great!" I said.

"Brendan would have put a scare up them."

"It would give him a good excuse for a fight, anyway," I said. "Make him feel a big man. That's just what Brendan is panting for."

"I wish Brendan had been there just the same," said Orla. "It is all right for you to talk, Nora Mullan. You don't know what it was like! I do."

"Don't say a word to Brendan or any of his lot about what happened," I warned Orla. "There'll only be a pack more trouble if you do."

"They put GOBBER GUN RULE on the sand," Orla said. "Do you think they've got guns?"

"Don't you go around suggesting the Gobbers have got guns, or Brendan will want one too!" I said.

"They've no right coming here and fighting us." Orla said. "Nobody would ever fight here if it wasn't for people coming in from outside."

I didn't argue about it at the time, but the more I thought about it, the surer I was that Orla was wrong, the trouble was in us to begin with. If it hadn't been the Gobbers, it would have been somebody else, somebody who was the least bit different from the rest of us, so that we could pick them out. That was what happened to the Spaniards, and the people who tried to build the pier. In a horrible way, it was also what was happening to Stella.

I didn't tell Orla, because I didn't think she would understand.

Seven

I knew Orla wouldn't be able to keep it to herself, and I was right. She says she didn't tell but being caught by the Gobbers was too good a story for her to resist it. She must have gone away and told someone, because the next thing that happened was that Brendan Egg called a Special Meeting.

Colum Rice came with the message. "You are to report at the sluice pipe at six o'clock sharp," he said. "Brendan and Damien are making a Defence Force. Well, Brendan is making it really, because he's the leader, but it was Damien's idea."

"What for?" I said. "Defence against what?"

"Against the Gobbers," he said, and he went off all excited.

I didn't go, but most of the other kids did, and the next day when I was in the playground at school Damien and Colum Rice and Marcus Toal and little James Rice came up and got me in the corner by the bike shed and Damien said:

"Are you with us or against us, Nora-No-Guts?"

"Don't you call me that," I said.

"Nora, Nora-No-Guts!" Colum chanted.

"I'm not No-Guts."

"Then you're with us, aren't you?" Damien said.

I didn't say a thing to him. I just walked away from them but James and Colum Rice got in front of me and stopped me.

"You'd better be with us, Nora," Damien said. "If you're not with us, you're against us."

"I'm not with anybody," I said.

"Right!" he said. "Then nobody's with you. Nobody will speak to you or have anything to do with you, Nora-No-Guts, because you are just a coward and traitor!"

Colum stuck out his tongue at me. James Rice spat at my feet. He wiped his mouth with the back of his hand and blew a raspberry in my face, and then he gave me a look and walked away.

"Don't let them upset you, Nora," Orla said.

"Why are they picking on me?" I said. "Why not you?"

Orla didn't say anything. She just looked awkward.

"I'm not supposed to speak to you," she said. "But I am because I am your friend, and I don't care what Brendan says."

"You're in his gang!" I said, and the way I said it must have told her how disgusting I thought it was.

"I'm not."

"Yes you are."

"I'm not. Not *exactly*," she was beginning to get confused. "I feel differently about it from you, that's all. I'm the one they came after, remember that. So I am for Brendan, in a way. I'm not joining his daft Defence Force or anything, but I'm not going to tell on him."

"You told him you were for him," I said, refusing to let her off the hook.

She didn't say a word.

"I'm fed up," I said. "I don't think you're much of a friend, ganging up on Brendan Egg's side."

"I'm not taking Brendan's side," she said. "Well, in a way I suppose I am, but it's either them or us, isn't it? If you're against Brendan, you're for the Gobbers. There's no half way house. They're Gobbers and city people and there was no fighting here till they came."

"Brendan broke James Ogle's arm," I said. "That was fighting. Anyway, it works the other way round. If you're with Brendan, you're against me. Brendan is against me, and he's going to stay against me because I'm not going round in his Defence Force having fights with Gobbers just because he wants to show what a big man he isn't."

"I'm for you," Orla said.

"Good." I was relieved, because I had no idea

what I was going to do if everybody was against me.

"I'm for you, but I'm not against Brendan," she said. "Nobody is, not even your Chris."

Chris?

"I don't believe you," I said.

Then I went looking for Chris, but I couldn't find him.

Chris was too small to be mixed up with Brendan. Stella would never let him. *I* would never let him.

I came back up the lane after school on my own, wondering miserably if I had just missed Orla, or if she was keeping out of my way like everybody else.

"Why so doleful, Nora?" Stella said, when I got in.

"Nothing," I said.

"You don't look as if it is nothing."

I gave a shrug.

I didn't want to tell her what was wrong. I would have told her if she had been my own mother, but she was just a trying-to-be-kind stranger, standing in until something better could be arranged. If my father got the job at the Field Centre or if he decided we had to move so he could go on the way he was, she would be away. I didn't want to talk to her or tell her anything about what I really thought, because tomorrow she might be gone.

Stella had the kettle on the range, and she gave me a cup of tea.

"Drink that," she said. "You look as if you need warming up."

"It's a cold day."

I should have seen the danger coming, but I missed it. I had my mind too much on the Nora-No-Guts business and being the Ballyhannis coward and traitor.

"You're bound to feel the cold if you don't wear your anorak in this weather," Stella said.

I didn't say anything.

"Why aren't you wearing it?"

"I haven't got it," I said.

"Haven't got it? Where is it?"

I looked at Stella. I could have told her some lie, and another day I might have, but I was feeling rotten enough inside with everybody getting at me, and I suppose I felt like a Christian thrown to the Lions. I didn't tell her a lie. I told her the truth.

"I left it on the island when I was out for the blackberries," I said, and the minute I said it I could have cut my tongue out.

"If that isn't typical!" Stella burst out, indignantly. "What do you think your father is, made of money?"

"I just forgot it," I said.

"Well, you can just remember it again! Put on your big jersey and go over to the island this

71

minute before the light goes, and see you bring it back with you," Stella said, and nothing I could say would put her off the notion.

"A good new coat like that!"

"It's not a good coat. It's an anorak."

"It's all you have to get you through the winter," she said.

Stella made me go. She made me go off to the island, where I didn't want to go, and I couldn't tell her *why* I didn't want to go, because the news that I was on the Gobbers Wanted List for setting my dog on Crystal would only have made her madder.

"Go! Now! Quick, before dark, while you can," Stella said.

Off I went.

Eight

I went over the causeway to Inishnagal on my own.

It wouldn't have been so frightening if I had had Erk for company, but in a way it might have been a bad idea. The Gobbers might have caught him, despite his teeth, and then the poor old thing might have been hurt. Anyway, I couldn't find him.

The feeling of being alone made me stick to the idea that I *had* to go.

All for an old anorak – an old *new* anorak, actually!

I went because everybody was against me, Stella and Mrs. McEntee and Brendan Egg and Colum and James and rotten Damien and even Orla, who was supposed to be my friend. I was the Ballyhannis traitor and coward and none of them wanted me and they were all more or less saying that I was some kind of dud, no use to anybody. I was in no mood to have Gobbers or anybody else say to me *You can't do this* or *You can't do that*. I was in trouble because I wouldn't buckle down and do what other people told me to, and if I didn't get the anorak because I was afraid of the Gobbers I would be doing just that.

The Gobbers weren't going to give me orders!

It was a brave enough idea and it grew in me going down the lane so that when I got to the shore I was buoyed up by the feel of it, the feeling that I was showing everyone. But by the time I was half way across the causeway my heart was in my mouth.

I will not go back and let them all laugh at me! I told myself, and I deliberately slowed myself down and tried to think about how to find the anorak.

I was sure it was somewhere in the bushes around the Spaniards' House. I'd left it there when I ran away – I absolutely refused to think about *why* I'd run away, because the Sighing just couldn't be true. I couldn't face that idea at all.

My anorak would be by the Spaniards' House if the Gobbers hadn't found it, or the sheep made a dinner of it. Would sheep eat an anorak? Would it kill them if they did? Old Mr. Cully would be mad at me if I killed one of his sheep for him.

I kept on thinking about the anorak and the sheep and what Mr. Cully might say and how much a dead sheep might cost and *anything* but what I was doing.

The Gobbers had a warning all ready for me.
GOBBER RULE
OKAY!

They were marking out their territory. Some-body had been at the rocks with an aerosol spray, in great big letters that were meant to be seen.

Our stones. The island stones. Not our stones, really. The Island of the Strangers, cut off from the rest of the Headland. I inspected their art-work.

BUGSY BRENNAN IS A BUTTERFLY CELTIC ARE THE CHAMPIONS SEAN and ALDO RULE

I came out on to the grass and up the hill towards the Spaniards' House, with the memory of my last visit there forcing itself to the front of my mind again. The Gobbers were bad enough without strangers from the past putting their oars in.

The gulls were mewing.

Never mind that it was a clear, bright evening, not the middle of the night. The idea of the murdered Spaniards sighing was held in check only by the fear of live Gobbers.

The Gobbers were sneaky. They might be watching me, a whole pack of them moving round behind the rocks to cut me off, so that I couldn't escape. Maybe that was what had disturbed the gulls.

The Gobbers couldn't do much to me anyway. It was all kid's stuff. But I could still have done without the rotten gulls shouting the odds. They made me think of massacres, which wasn't what I wanted to think about, just then.

The grass was well cropped where the sheep had been at it, and springy-spongy beneath my feet. That was good, because it meant that I made no noise, but the higher I got up the slope towards the Spaniards' House the more exposed I was, right up on top of the Gull Cliff.

I wasn't going to turn back, that was one sure thing. I had to get my anorak, or Stella would bite my ears off. My father couldn't afford to go buying new anoraks all the time. I decided that I wasn't doing what I was doing for Stella, or to show everybody that I wasn't a coward and a traitor; I was doing what I was doing for my father, so that he wouldn't have to buy me a new anorak that we couldn't afford.

I kept that idea in my head, and I ran the last bit up towards the old crumbly rocks by the Spaniards' House and the Gull Cliff.

It was easy enough to find the place where I had trampled the brambles with my wellingtons, but there was no sign of my anorak. I though it might have blown away, but I couldn't see it. It should have been easy enough to see because there was only the green of the bushes and the black stone of the Spaniards' House to look at, and my anorak is red.

I couldn't find it.

"Looking for something?"

I spun round, but the voice wasn't coming from behind me.

"Up here!" she jeered.

It was the girl, Crystal. She was up above me on one of the rocks.

I might have known. After all, the gulls had warned me.

"You want to watch yourself up there," I said. "The cliff is loose."

"Oh yeh?" she said.

She WOULD be the one to spot me! She was the sort of kid you would expect to find wandering around exploring, instead of doing Gobber things with the others. Maybe she didn't get on with them because she was the only skin head, or maybe she turned herself into the only skin head because she didn't get on with them . . .

"I know your name," she said. "Your name's Nora Mullan."

"So?"

"How'd I know your name?"

I didn't know how she knew my name. I didn't much care, either. Maybe Orla had told her. How she knew my name didn't bother me in the least, but it was meant to, I could tell that from the way she said it. She was crouched up on the rocks looking pleased with herself.

"Okay," I said. "How'd you know my name then?"

"Read it," she said. "Read it in your coat."

"My anorak?"

"Your red coat. I read it on the wee tab. I know your name, Nora Mullan!"

"I want my anorak, please," I said, trying to keep the shake of temper out of my voice. I was bigger than she was, but she might be tougher.

"If you've got my coat and you don't give it back to me that's stealing," I said.

"Get a policeman," she said, standing up and edging herself down the rocks.

"Are you going to give it to me?" I said, as she came off in a shower of loose fragments.

"Where's your dog?"

I knew she was afraid of Erk. I wished I'd brought him!

"I'll bring him and get you," I said, and even I wasn't convinced.

"You will *like sugar*," she said, scornfully.

"Look," I said. "I'll fight you if I have to. I'm a very good fighter."

I was very angry inside. If she had done something to my anorak I had a good mind to tear her apart.

"So'm I," she said.

"Just give me my coat," I said.

"Oh yeh!"

"Give me my coat!" I advanced on her.

"Yeh!"

"Yeh" didn't mean yes, or anything like it. She was enjoying herself, annoying me. I couldn't go on saying give-me-my-coat but I managed it one more time.

"Give it to me, *please*," I said.

"*Please?*" she mocked.

"Yes. *Please*," I said.

"I wouldn't say please to you, not for anything," she said.

I couldn't hold back any longer! I lunged at her and I got her by the shoulders and I was banging her against the wall and then she stuck her foot round my leg and tripped me. I was going over and then I came down a terrible crack against the wall.

I had a big black pain in my head.

"Hey," someone was pulling at me. "Hey, you, Nora."

I tried to say leave me alone, but I didn't manage it.

"You're all bloody," Crystal said.

I was lying on the ground and she was bending over me and *she* was all bloody, that was the first thing I noticed. There was blood down the front of her denim jacket, and then I put my hand up to my nose and it came away sticky and I realised I was the one that was bleeding, and she was bloody with my blood.

I think the blood must have frightened her.

"Put your head back," she said.

"And choke to death," I mumbled. "You'd like that."

I sat up. My head was sore, and the blood was dripping out of me. I've never seen so much blood, and it wouldn't stop.

"Don't you go fainting on me," she said. "Here," she was bending over me, but she wasn't trying to get at me, not any more. She put her hands beneath my shoulders, and she shrugged me up against the rock. "You look sick," she said. "Are you going to be sick?"

I shook my head, but she was right. I had a sick feeling inside me, and it wasn't just the blood.

"We do judo in our school," she said.

That was great. I was supposed to be all pleased for her.

"Are you all right?" she asked. "You're not concussed or anything?"

"No." I was feeling my head, and still feeling awful inside. I closed my eyes.

"Just take in a few big breaths," she said. "You banged your head on the stone."

I concentrated on what I was doing.

"You're bleeding," she said.

I felt like telling her I was no kind of a fool, of course I was bleeding. If I wasn't bleeding what was all that red stuff doing? There was blood enough for both of us.

"D'you often bleed?"

"Just the nose."

"Is it just your nose?"

"Your nose would bleed too if you cracked it on a rock," I said, impatiently.

"You mind who you pick fights with in future," she said.

It was on the tip of my tongue to tell her that her judo hadn't done her much good when the boys got her, but I didn't bother. I took the hanky she offered and stuffed it against my nose and mumbled: "Just let me bleed to death, will you?"

"I'll get your coat," she said.

I looked at her, not sure which way to take it. Maybe the blood had changed her tune.

"D'you not want your coat?" she said.

And then she did a weird thing. She moved down to the gable end, knelt down, and somehow squeezed herself in where it met the rock. It was like a disappearing act. One moment she was there, and the next she wasn't.

I went over to see what she'd done.

The shelf of rock came down right behind the house. There was a great big overlap, and layers of it right across, like a cut cake, horizontal. Only one of the layers wasn't a layer, but a dark fissure in the rock. One of her legs was disappearing inside it.

"Come out of that!" I said, terribly frightened. The old soft rock and shale was too dangerous for games like that.

"Getting the coat!" her muffled voice said.

I went down on my knees to look into the gap, and there she was, only it wasn't as risky as it looked, because there was strong grey rock around her, not the loose shale of the cliff. She had my coat.

"Here," she said. "Grab that, and pull me out."

I took hold of my anorak, and grabbed half on to it and half on to her, and got her out.

"Good hidey place!" she said.

I looked at it, thinking.

"I stuffed your coat down," she said. "I saw you coming and I hid it."

I was still looking at the gap in the rock.

"Now you've got the coat, you'd better clean yourself up before you go home," she said.

We went down the sheep ground and on to the rocks facing the headland, where we found a salt water pool. The red blood spreading on the water when she rinsed her jacket out was really something.

"This makes us blood brothers," I said, looking at it.

"Sisters," she said. "Will you get home all right?"

"I'll get home," I said, although I was still

feeling a bit dizzy. Nose bleeds are like that, when you lose a lot of blood.

"Mr. Brennan would help you," she said.

"I don't need any help."

I got to my feet. My head was sore, and the front of my jersey was wet, and my nostrils were stinging from the salt. I still had to hold her hanky up to my nose.

"I'm Crystal Reilly," she said.

I knew she was called Crystal anyway, she didn't have to tell me.

"Well," she said. "You'd better get back before any of the others spot you."

I looked at her.

"I don't want to get you into trouble," I said.

"I don't get on with them, that's all," she answered. "I should have stayed at home."

"I'd better not get caught then," I said.

I was on my way across the rocks to the causeway when she shouted after me. "Hey! Hey, Nora! Hey!"

"What?"

"Don't forget your anorak!"

"No chance," I said.

"Listen," she said. "Don't come back."

"I'll come back if I want to," I said.

"They're tough," she said.

"Who is tough?"

"*Them*," she said. "As tough as your ones, any day."

I left her on the shore, and found my way back over the causeway, all blood and blocked nostrils and annoyance with myself, but at least I'd got what I came for.

There was a reception committee waiting for me on the other side.

Brendan and Marcus and Colum and our Chris.

They were on the wall outside Egg's Shop when I came off the shore.

"Gobber Girl!" Colum said.

I gave him a look. They had obviously seen me with Crystal on the rocks.

"Good friends, are you?" Brendan said. "You and the Gobbers?"

"Chris?" I said, ignoring him. "Time you were coming home, Chris."

Chris looked at Brendan. I'd said it the wrong way. It looked as if I was ordering him to come home, doing my Big Sister act.

"You know the score now, Chris," Brendan said.

"Gobber Girl!" Colum said.

I felt sorry for Chris, but I was blind with rage at him at the same time. I am his sister. He ought to have been on my side, even if I was mixed up with the Gobbers, which I wasn't, and even if he was scared of Brendan.

Scared or not, he would have to decide between us.

"Coming, Chris?" I said again.

"Don't answer her, Chris," said Colum. "She's a Gobber Girl."

Chris had gone pale.

"I'll . . . I'll be up in a minute," he said, but he mumbled it, and he didn't look at me, and he didn't come after me although I walked slowly up the lane, giving him every chance.

I was ashamed of him, and ashamed of me, too. I should have . . . then I tried to figure out *what* I was ashamed of. I'd got the anorak, and that was what I had set out to do. If Chris was too scared to side up with his own sister then he knew what he could go and do.

Nine

I was at the Spaniards' House and there was something trying to get me, something that was oozing out of the dark split in the rock.

It was tall and bright and glittery yellow like bad butter and it had a head and shoulders and arms but no face and no hands and there were big holes in its head where its eyes should have been and it was blind and groping and sighing and I knew if it touched me I was dead.

"Nora! Nora!"

It withered away, back down into the narrow split in the face of the rock and I was being shaken, and shaken, and I was awake.

"Nora!" Stella said. "Are you all right, Nora?"

I was in my own bed, and there was no yellow thing and no split in the rock face. I was in my own bed in my house and I could see Stella and hear Stella, but I was still damp with the fear of it getting me.

"Don't let it get me, Stella," I said.

"There," she said. "There now, Nora!" And I felt the warmth of her as she cradled me up against her body. "It's all right, Nora. Nothing's going to get you while I'm here."

I was crying. I didn't want to cry, but I was crying.

"Come on here now," she said.

She lifted me out of bed. I am a big lump, too big for carrying, but she must have been stronger than I thought, for she got me down the stairs and into my father's chair and I was by the fire and Stella was with me in the glow of it.

"Are you all right now, Nora?" she asked.

I nodded.

"Cup of tea?"

"That'd be nice."

She went into the kitchen, first putting her wrap round me. When she came back with the tea she was wearing her going-out coat over her nightdress.

"You scared the heart out of me, Nora," she said.

"I scared the heart out of me!" I said, trying to make a joke of it, but it hadn't been funny, not at the time, with the yellow thing oozing from the rock like a worm, out to nab me.

"There was a big thing coming to get me," I said, and I managed a grin to show her I knew it was daft. I had a feeling I was too big to be having bogey man nightmares like that.

"Nothing is going to get you," she said.

I *knew* nothing was going to get me. I was in our front room, in front of the fire which she had raked up from the embers. I couldn't have felt safer.

"I'm not scared now," I said.

"No," she said. "Have a drink of your tea."

She settled down in the chair opposite me and I drank the tea, looking at her. She is a big, girl – not a girl, a woman. Her hair was soft around her, and glistening red brown in the fire light, and her eyes were gentle, and I was sorry for some of the things I'd said and thought about her. She was only trying to be good to me, and I must have been a terrible nuisance considering the way I kept getting into trouble.

"Stella," I said.

"Yes?" She looked up at me, putting her cup down at the stool beside her feet. She had her old green slippers on, and they looked odd beneath her good coat.

"Are you going to marry my Daddy, Stella?" I asked.

She didn't say anything for a long time. She raked the fire, and put the tongs back on their rest with a clang.

"I might," she said. "Would you mind?"

I shook my head.

"Sure?"

"It's all right, if you want to," I said.

"Well, I want to."

I didn't ask her if *he* wanted to. I knew he did. He hadn't told me. Nobody told me, and for once I hadn't accidentally on purpose overheard anything, either. I just knew, and it was better now that she knew I knew. It had been a bad thing between us, and now it was a good thing.

"Then you'd stay with us always?" I said.

"You are sure you don't mind, aren't you, Nora?" She was looking into the firelight. "I wouldn't try to replace your mother, or anything."

She looked up at me.

"I know I couldn't do that," she said.

She was right. She was being fair, and she was trying not to hurt me.

"Maybe we won't fight so much now," she said.

I got up and I went over and I gave her a kiss and she got hold of me and she hugged me and both of us were nearly in tears.

"Pair of softies!" Stella said. She got her hanky out of the pocket of her good coat and blew her nose, and it sounded like a fog horn. She has a big nose with a bump on it, and she isn't really beautiful, it was just the firelight flickering that made her look so nice – and the niceness in her.

"Will we tell Chris?" I said.

"No," she said. "Your father's coming home to see about the job at the Field Centre. Your father will tell him."

When I went back to bed I didn't sleep for a

long time, trying to work out what was in my head and what I really thought about it.

I loved Stella but I had a feeling that, if I'd been bigger, I might have been able to look after Chris and my father myself, and it might have been better, but it might not. She wouldn't go away if they got married, and we would be a proper family. Maybe I could help her with her own work. If I could arrange things so that she got more time for her books, instead of worrying her all the time, it would be great. Maybe if I told her I would do the dinners she would be pleased. Maybe . . .

I got lost in the maybes and went to sleep.

Ten

I went down the lane to school with Chris the next morning. He didn't say anything about what had happened at Egg's Corner the night before, and neither did I, but when we got to the bend he went on ahead and in through the school gate on his own.

I knew who was the traitor all right, and it wasn't me!

I went into the school yard. Marcus Toal was there, and Roisin and the two Morgans and some of the others. Damien and Colum were by the toilets. They all stopped what they were doing and watched me.

I wasn't going to let them have the satisfaction! I went straight through the pack of them and into the classroom.

There were big chalked letters on the blackboard.

I just stood there, looking at them.

I'm not going to say what was written up on the board about me. Looking at it was bad enough.

There was a giggle at the door. I spun round.

They were all at the door, pressing round it to see what I would do.

I stood and looked at them. I was feeling sick inside.

Damien put out his tongue at me.

I went for him! I got him by the hair and I was banging his rotten head against the open door and he was screeching blue murder and then Mrs. McEntee came in early.

"Nora!"

I let go of Damien's hair.

He was crying and I was glad he was crying, even if it was going to get me into trouble.

"Nora!" she was about to go for me, and then she stopped. Her eyes had taken in the rest of the classroom, and that included what was written on the board.

Her mouth snapped shut.

"Go to your places," she said.

She went up to the dais at the front of the room and got out the duster. She cleaned every last speck of chalk off the board and then she turned back to us, banging the duster down on her desk.

What was she going to say?

"Time for our prayers," she said.

We all got up with a lot of shuffling, and we said our prayers.

"Get your books out," she said.

We got our books out, and she went on with

the lesson as if nothing had happened. I was sitting up at the front desk on my own, because it was Orla's day for the dentist, and I never looked behind me once.

The lesson went on until breaktime, and at breaktime she called me back.

"Well, Nora?" she said.

"Sorry, Miss," I said.

"Perhaps you would like to tell me what this is all about?"

I said nothing.

"Was it Damien Hughes?" she said.

"I don't know, Miss," I said.

"If you are going to attack people like that you'd better know. It was somebody at this school, was it, Nora?" she asked. I knew what she was thinking. Brendan Egg is the one who uses words like that most. It would have been easy enough for Brendan to get in to our classroom.

"Damien stuck out his tongue at me, Miss. I just got mad."

"I didn't ask you that, Nora. I asked who wrote those things about you on the board? I'd also like to know why they were written?"

I stood where I was. It was bad enough them writing things on the board about me, now I was getting the scolding for it as well. If I told Mrs. McEntee the whole story, I would be proving everyone right.

"I want to think about what I'm going to do, Nora," she said, when I didn't make any reply. "Perhaps I should have a word with Stella."

"Don't tell Stella, Miss!"

I didn't want Stella to know. Not now, when things were going right between us. The last thing in the world that I wanted at that moment was a fuss with Stella. She would get upset and write to my father and I would be spoiling everything for them.

"Ask Damien Hughes to come in here to see me, please, Nora," Mrs. McEntee said.

I got Damien.

"Sneak!" he said.

"I never," I said.

We went back into the classroom. Damien had gone red as a beetroot.

"Well, Damien?" she said.

"I never did it, Miss," he said, but all the bounce had gone out of him. Mr. Hughes is a cross man, and when he loses his temper he takes it out on Damien. Damien was afraid he would get a note home.

"I think you know who did, Damien," said Mrs. McEntee.

Damien got redder.

"I never did it, Miss," he repeated.

"And your lips are sealed?" Mrs. McEntee asked.

"Yes, Miss."

"If there is any repetition of this there's going to be big trouble. Do you understand that, the pair of you?"

"Yes, Miss."

"Right. Now, Nora, will you apologise to Damien for hurting him like that?"

It was on the tip of my tongue to say that I wouldn't, because it was his own fault that he got his hair pulled and his head banged, and I only hoped it had hurt him, but I didn't. I knew if I didn't apologise she would send up the lane for Stella.

"Sorry, Damien." I said.

"Damien?"

"I never done nothing, Miss," Damien protested.

"*Damien?*"

"Sorry," he said, but he didn't sound it.

"Look at Nora when you say it, Damien. Again, please!"

"Sorry, Nora," Damien said, and by this time he was crimson.

When we got out into the playground afterwards he told me he wasn't one bit sorry.

"Just because you've got old Miss on your side it doesn't mean you're going to get away with anything, Nora," he said.

I sat on the wall. I couldn't see Chris about. The only one who said anything to me was Sally

Colley who came up and told me what one of the words meant.

"Everybody knows that," I said.

"It's dirty," she said. "You're dirty if you know it, Nora!" and off she went.

Still, at least she was someone to talk to.

I talked to nobody else till I went home.

Orla was waiting for me, round the bend in the lane where no one from school could see her.

"Nora-Nora-Nora," she mumbled. She mumbled because the side of her face was still swollen from her visit to the dentist. She was looking pale and puffy.

"How are your teeth?" I asked, trying to make my voice sound not-too-friendly, because if she wanted to be on my side she should have come out and shown everybody, not hidden away up the lane.

"I'm all sore and Mammy says I'm to stay in the house and go to bed," she said.

"So here you are," I said. "That's logical!"

"I only came because of you," she said.

Poor Orla. There was a lot of cotton wool stuck in her mouth and her lip was swollen up like a banana.

"What have I done?" I asked.

"Damien told your Chris that Brendan Egg was going to shoot Erk."

I stopped in my tracks.

"Shoot Erk? What with?"

"A gun."

"Brendan hasn't got a gun."

"Damien says he's made one."

"To shoot Erk with?" I was still grappling with the idea. I couldn't believe it. I couldn't believe in Brendan Egg with a gun, and I certainly didn't believe he would shoot Erk.

"Brendan likes Erk," I said. "He used to give him bacon rinds from the shop."

"Damien told your Chris that Brendan would shoot Erk if Chris didn't do what he was told."

"Oh," I said.

"The whole gang of them are going to the island this evening, and Damien said Chris had to come too, or Brendan would shoot Erk."

"He was pulling Chris's leg," I said. I felt sore at Damien just the same, for telling our little Chris a thing like that that would really scare him. Chris would believe that Brendan had made a gun all right, and he would never work out that Brendan is the last person to go round shooting other people's dogs. Brendan is just like Chris about animals.

"Probably he was," mumbled Orla.

She sounded doubtful. I knew what it was. She'd come out Nora-Nora-Nora-ing with her Big Story, and I was making her look silly again, Orla knows I don't take her Nora-Nora-Nora stories seriously.

I thought I'd give her an Orla-Orla-Orla story

to make up for it. Then she could go home and Mammy-Mammy-Mammy it to her mother, and that would send her to bed happy, even if it wasn't true. I didn't know whether the story was true or not, but I'd been thinking about it — I'd had nothing to do but think, since nobody would talk to me – and I thought it *might* be true, and that was good enough for an Orla-Orla-Orla story.

"I've got a story for you," I said.

"What?" she said, taking the cotton wool out of her mouth and looking at it. It was all yellow with that pain killing stuff the dentist uses.

"Inishnagal," I said. "I've found where the Spaniard hid."

"Have you?" Orla's eyes opened wide.

I had her listening to me now.

"Yes," I said, trying to make it sound impressive. "In the course of my Investigations into The Mystery of Where the Spaniard Hid I have uncovered the Secret of that Age Old Riddle!"

"What did you find?" She'd forgotten all about her sore teeth.

"There's a kind of crack in the rock, low down, behind the back wall of the Spaniards' House," I said. "I think a man could squeeze into it and lie there. Nobody'd ever see it unless they knew it was there."

"You did," she objected.

"Well, it's very difficult to find," I said. "It's the way the rock folds. You wouldn't know there is a gap until you're looking right into it." I didn't want to tell her about Crystal finding it, because that would only start her off about Gobbers and I'd had enough on that particular subject.

"You think the Spaniard hid in a hole in the rock?"

"It's more a long crack," I said. "You'd have to force yourself in, sideways."

"I like the story about turning into a gull better," said Orla. "He was a Spanish Witch, and he turned himself into a gull and flew above them, calling on the souls of the dead ones. That's much more interesting."

"Truth isn't always interesting," I said.

"It's just that I like ghostie stories," said Orla.

"You don't look well," I said.

"I'm sick. I'm probably dying," Orla said. "I'm going home to bed. If I don't die, I'll see you tomorrow!"

"And if you do, you can come and haunt me instead," I said.

I went up to our house, thinking about Orla's story about Erk, and about Brendan's gun.

It was typical of Orla's stories, she would believe almost anything. The trouble was that people then believed her, and the more they believed her the more she believed herself, even

99

the bits that she knew she'd added on. That was exactly what Damien wanted to happen! He knew Orla would tell me the full technicolor version, and I was supposed to get all scared and make a fuss and then everyone would laugh at me.

It would serve them all right if I told Stella everything.

But there was no Stella to tell, just a note, propped up on Stella's typewriter.

NORA
Had to go to Belfast
Good-Good-Good news.
Dinner in the oven.
If you need anything go
down to Egg's. Mrs. E. is
looking out for you.
Love
Stella

I was a latch key kid, like Damien Hughes!

You should have seen my dinner. It was bacon and cabbage and it was all soggy. I didn't eat much of it. Just because Stella got good news about her grant coming through or something I wasn't going to eat soggy bacon. I made myself some cheese sandwiches instead.

Chris gets out of school at two o'clock so she had probably taken him with her. I gave Erk his dinner, though he left the cabbage as well, and then I started to think about things.

Brendan Egg hadn't got a gun, and if he had he wouldn't shoot Erk. Brendan likes Erk. Brendan bandaged up Erk's leg the time when it was caught in the wire down by the sluice pipe.

It was all a Get-Nora campaign, with Damien and Brendan working it out between them, using Chris, and Orla's gossip. If Chris went out to the island with them they would make sure he would get into any trouble that was going.

Anyway it couldn't happen because Chris had gone off with Stella. But had he?

I didn't know that, not for certain. Where would he be, if he wasn't with Stella? He could be at the harbour fooling around with Damien and the others, though that didn't seem likely. If he'd been close to home he would have taken Erk with him . . . unless he was still worried about Damien's story. Stella might have left him with somebody. That posed a problem. If he was at one of the other houses round the Headland, he might show up for the raid on the island, and I wouldn't know a thing about it!

I could go down the lane and tell Mrs. Egg. "Your Brendan is scaring our Chris by saying he'll shoot Erk."

It didn't sound convincing. Brendan would say he was only teasing, or deny it altogether. Maybe Brendan didn't know about it, and it was all Damien's invention, or Orla getting things wrong. I was all confused. Brendan isn't a bad person. He isn't good either. Brendan wanted some excitement and that was what the Gobbers and the Get-Nora-Campaign added up to.

If I went down to Mrs. Egg I would look silly in the end, especially if Chris was away with Stella.

She might have mentioned Chris in her note. *His* dinner wasn't soggy in the oven, so he'd either eaten it or Stella had sent him off somewhere else.

It was all Stella's fault.

No it wasn't. That was just me on my mix up of thoughts about Stella again. Stella was being nice and easy going as usual, never thinking I might worry about Chris, because of course she didn't know about the plans to raid the island.

I had a problem.

Supposing Orla was *right*? If Brendan and his Defence Force were going over to rip the Gobbers' minibus tyres or muck about with their tents or something there *might* be trouble, and Chris *might* be mixed up in it. I didn't want that to happen, but I didn't see how I could prevent it without giving them all a big laugh at me. Damien and Brendan would just love it if I fell for Orla's stupid story.

I hid myself at Slaughter Point where I could see and not be seen. The idea was that from my hiding place I could keep an eye on the causeway. If nothing happened they wouldn't know that I'd been on a fool's errand, but if they went over to the island I would know about it.

It was very cold, and in the back of my head was the thought that Chris was probably sitting indoors somewhere with Stella, while I was out at the end of the Headland, freezing.

A crowd of them came down to the shore.

That was when I realised that I'd made a mistake. From Slaughter Point I couldn't see Brendan's lot passing the light at Egg's Corner, and once they were on the shore it was too dark to make out who was who. I could make out Brendan and Damien in the lead, but the others were just dark shadows, making their way over to the causeway. Was Chris with them?

There was nothing I could do but follow them to find out.

Eleven

Brendan may have seen himself as a new Owen Leary, leading his men on to the island to massacre the strangers, but he wasn't much good at it.

His army made too much noise for one thing. I had absolutely no difficulty in keeping track of them, even in the dusk, and every time Brendan ordered somebody to shut up his voice was louder than all the rest put together.

I was hoping Mr. Brennan would hear them and scare them off, but he didn't.

Brendan led them through the rocks, down towards the pier end, where the Gobbers had their camp. I came after them, keeping my distance because the last thing I wanted was to get caught up in a fight between the Gobbers and the Defence Force. I was beginning to feel hopeful that Chris wasn't with them, because I felt sure I would have recognised his voice. Unfortunately, I couldn't be certain, so I had to keep going.

I worked out the way they were going and decided to take a chance and bolt across the open sheep ground so that I could get close enough to the Gobber's camp to see what was happening.

I found a good position among the rocks, and crouched there with the Gobbers' tents just below me, to my right.

There was no sign of the Gobbers, just the faint glimmer of the embers of a fire. They must have gone off on one of their night observations with Mr. Brennan.

I thought I saw someone moving, at the edge of the firelight.

I changed my position for a better view. It was a boy. A little boy. Chris? No, it wasn't Chris, it was James Rice with his jersey pulled up to cover his face like a gangster on T.V.

By now I was almost certain that Chris wasn't with them. There were more shadows gathering round the Gobber' minibus! I heard them opening the doors at the back, and then I heard the tinkle of breaking glass.

They were smashing Mr. Brennan's specimen jars.

They were also making a lot of noise dancing about and enjoying themselves as they did it.

Then they stopped breaking things, and a lot of the shadows came together in a sort of circle, and I heard Damien arguing.

I was so interested trying to make out what was going on that I didn't see the Gobbers.

One minute there were just the few shadows beside the minibus, and the next there was a sound like a war whoop and a whole lot of Gobbers came charging across the camp site.

Brendan's lot took one look and ran. The Gobbers were much bigger than the Ballyhannis Defence Force, and we all knew it.

The trouble was that Brendan and Damien led them up through the rocks, straight toward the spot where I was hiding. The only thing I could do was to start running too!

I headed back for the causeway, but I didn't get far, for I found I was heading straight for a big bunch of Gobbers, who had cut off the retreat. I couldn't get back to the causeway, so I turned and plunged in amongst the rocks. There were so many rocks it was like a maze, and my only hope was to get lost in them. I was dodging and weaving like mad. Then somebody started throwing stones. One zinged off just above my head and I heard somebody give a yowl, which didn't help because it directed the Gobbers over our way. Everybody was all muddled up in the rocks, Gobbers and our kids, the trouble was that the Gobbers were so much bigger than everybody but Brendan that getting caught meant getting done.

I knew one person who wasn't getting caught. Me!

They weren't going to catch me because I knew the best hiding place on the island. That was where I headed for.

I got up to the Spaniards' House, running doubled up. I hesitated just for a minute, not really wanting to go down into the dark split in the rock; for all I knew it might be full of dead Spaniards. I hadn't long to think about it, because there was a lot of shouting coming from the rocks behind me. It was my best chance of escape, possibly my only one.

It was easy enough when Crystal did it, but at first I couldn't even find how she'd got in. I got part way in, and then I stuck, neither in nor out! The voices were getting nearer. I wriggled, and worked myself down the crack in the rock, and suddenly it wasn't so difficult. I had one hand out, against the back wall of the Spaniards' House, and with that and my knee I was able to shove down. The fissure ran on into the rock, all right, but it was very narrow. If the Spaniard had hidden in it, he must have been a very small Spaniard. I shoved and pushed a bit more, and then I got my head in, and got a bit of purchase on the rock, and suddenly I was through the crack, flat on my face, but able to move freely.

That's what I thought! I lifted my head, and *crack!* It was a hidey hole, all right, but a very small one. There wasn't more than nine centimetres above my head.

I moved, and my movement brushed some of the small stones where I was lying – and that was where I changed my mind about the nice safe hidey hole.

It wasn't a nice safe hidey hole at all. I heard the stones rattle away from me, going down, and down and down, and the next minute something gave way, and I was going after them, slithering and sliding on damp rock in the darkness. I tried to pull myself up, but the rock was wet and slippy, and it was frightening in the darkness. I began to panic. I could hear the sea, a long way away below, and I knew that one slip and I'd be down in it. I groped around in the dark, and found a purchase, and the next minute I was heaving myself up, determined that Gobbers or no Gobbers I was getting out!

I managed it. I crawled out, and lay against the wall, and there was a lot of shouting going on, so I kept against the wall. But the shouting wasn't about me.

It was Brendan.

He was up on the rocks, framed against the night sky. And there was someone else up there with him. It was the boy Crystal didn't like, Aldo.

They were having a fight, and they'd stopped.

Or they were about to have a fight, I didn't know which. I did know it was a terribly dangerous place for them to be, because another metre and they'd be over the edge taking half the old shale cliff with them on their way down to the rocks below.

"Got you!" Aldo said.

There were other Gobbers, three or four of them, all ganging up on Brendan. I moved away from the wall, to see if I could get clear.

"Going to stay up there all night?" Aldo sneered.

"You come near me, any of you, and I'll chuck you over the cliff, so I will!" Brendan shouted at him.

He wasn't silly. If they had any wit at all they could see that only one at a time could get at him up there, and on the old crumbly rock anything might happen.

"Cockshie!" someone said.

There was a rattle, and I heard Brendan give a grunt of pain. A big stone came down the side of the rock. It was more of a rock than a stone. They were heaving rocks at him, aiming to drive him down.

"Stop it! You stop it!" It was Crystal's voice. I saw her standing up and yelling. "Stop it! Stop! D'you hear me! Stop it!"

Nobody's going to pay any heed to her,

I thought, but then it seemed as though they had, because the stones stopped flying.

"He's got a gun," somebody said.

Brendan had a gun. It took a minute for me to take it in.

A gun!

He was standing up now, pointing it at them, his feet placed uncertainly on the side of the rock, his body pressed against it for balance. It didn't look like a proper gun, it was all funny, with a big long barrel that looked like a piece of lead pipe.

"I'll shoot!" he said, in a shaky voice. "First one throws anything, I'll shoot."

I was afraid he would fire off his old home-made gun. If he did, someone might be killed, and he would be a murderer. He wasn't watching me, he was looking in the other direction, at the Gobbers. I couldn't let Brendan be a murderer.

"You put that down at once, Brendan Egg!" I shouted, getting to my feet.

He turned his head at the sound of my voice and the next moment *zonk!*

The Gobber's stone hit him on the back of his head, and he dropped the gun and went down on to his knees, holding his head. At the same moment I saw Aldo reach out, pick up the gun and point it at Brendan and I knew he was going to shoot our Brendan. I did the only thing I could think of. I grabbed the nearest stone and I threw it at Aldo with all the force I could manage. I missed and he moved the gun, pointed it at me and pressed the trigger.

There was a big bang.

I could feel the bullet going in me.

But there was no bullet.

Instead, Aldo was staggering backwards clutching the remains of Brendan's rotten old home-made gun, which had exploded in his hands.

"Aldo!" Crystal yelled.

Aldo was gone. He took one step backwards, his face distorted with pain and shock and bewilderment, and then he went over the edge.

He didn't scream or anything.

It was weird. Like a picture, in slow motion. He disappeared, silently, and then, seconds later, there was a horrible soggy thump, followed by a lot of screeching from the gulls.

"Aldo," Crystal said. "Aldo!"

"Get!" somebody shouted.

One minute there were Gobbers there, and the next they were all running away down the rocks, frightened to be involved in it.

"Aldo's dead," said Crystal.

Brendan was on his feet. He was white as a ghost, and really scared. He looked as if he was going to be sick. He was shivering, and there was a trickle of blood from the back of his head, where the stone had hit him.

"You and your old gun!" I said, nearly crying myself. He'd only made the gun to show off to Damien and Colum, and now it had killed somebody.

"Aldo's dead," Crystal kept repeating.

"Get their teacher, Brendan," I said. "Get Mr. Brennan. Quick. We might be able to do something."

"He's gone," said Crystal. "One of your guys severed an artery breaking our jars. Brennan is away off to get him to a doctor."

We stood looking at each other. We were the ones who needed a doctor.

"Aldo's dead," said Crystal, again.

"Get somebody," I said. "You go and get help."

She went, but she would be too late. I knew that.

"He's not dead," said Brendan, almost shouting. "Maybe he's not. You don't know that." His voice trailed away. He knew as well as I did that even if Aldo had survived the fall, there was no way we could get down to him on the rocks. It would take us hours to get there over the rocks, and we would probably all be drowned anyway.

"The sea'll get him if he's not done for already," I said.

Right at that moment I heard the sea.

It wasn't the usual sound the sea makes, but a much more frightening one. It was the sound of the sea echoing up through the fissure in the rock, feeding back on its own echo . . . *sighing*.

Then I knew that there *was* a way to reach Aldo.

Twelve

It was horrible.

The rock was cold and wet and crumbly and I was caught there against it, groping my way downward towards the sighing sea. It was totally dark, as if I was in some nightmare where I was blind. I thought that I might never get out of that crack in the rock. I knew I was mad being there at all, but if I couldn't get down to the boy on the rocks we would all be murderers.

I could hear Brendan cursing in the darkness above me. He didn't fit. There was no way he could squeeze his big body through the gap in the rock.

It was me, or nobody.

Me, clinging on a rock face in the darkness, with the flesh scraped off my hands, wanting to go back, and knowing there was no way I could get back, because I'd already slithered and slipped too far.

If the Spaniard had escaped down the hole I was in, he must have been a dab hand at climbing.

I tried another move, and again I was sliding. I grabbed out in the dark, steadied myself, got my foot down on something, and felt around.

My foot got jammed, and I had another moment of panic . . . jammed, jammed right down in the middle of a rock, in a narrow crack where nobody would be able to get at me, with only Brendan knowing I was there.

"Nora, Nora!" he was shouting, up above. He'd lost his head altogether. He was no use to me.

I had to get my foot free. I screwed my body downward, and went over on my side. I was on something soft – sand.

There was light.

It was only a dim light, but after the pitch dark of the descent it was marvellous. *Light!*

I was at the bottom of the crack in the rock. I wriggled my foot free, bending round and straining against the stone, and then I started toward the light, squeezing and pushing and thrusting my way along the narrow channel in the rock.

There was an opening – I was out.

It was great. I was in the open, with the gulls rising from the rocks around me . . . and then I had a sickening shock.

I wasn't where I'd thought I'd be. I wasn't at the bottom of the Gull Cliff at all. I was nearer the top, in a crevice among the old crumbly rock, with the sea thirty metres or more below me.

I could have cried!

There was no reason why the crack in the rock *should* lead me down to the foot of the cliffs. I'd heard the sea, and worked out that I was going to be a big heroine and go down for Aldo. Instead here I was in need of a rescue myself.

I clung on to the cliff, cold and shivering, with every bit of me scratched and torn by my struggle in the rock fissure, knowing I'd had it.

No!

I was more than half way down. There was nothing for it, but to keep going.

It wasn't a sheer cliff. It wasn't really a cliff at all. It was a terribly steep crumbling rock face, and every time I moved I felt it was going to give way around me, but I went on, clawing and clinging and working my way down, closer and closer to the sound of the sea.

I must have been crying. My breath was coming in great gulps. There was blood trickling down my arms and I was all over sore, but so sore that I couldn't feel it. There was a numbness in the foot I had trapped in the crevice, and my fingers were stiff.

The old crumbly face was giving way. I made a grab, but I caught nothing. I was going over, backwards – going to break my back on the rocks below, and then I felt a great blow on my side and the next minute I was up to my waist in water. It broke over me, and pummelled me against the rocks . . . as if I wasn't pummelled enough.

Drown. I was going to drown.

But I *wasn't*, because I was sitting up in the water. The water was running away from me. And then it turned and surged back and I was lifted and scraped against the rock and I grabbed at the rock and caught it and clung on.

The water went back.

I was still there and it swept over me twice more before I could make the last push and get myself clear.

I huddled in against the rocks.

Aldo was lying about five metres away from me. He was on his back, like somebody sun-bathing, except that he was in his clothes, and his body from the waist down was in the sea.

"Aldo! Aldo!"

The croak of my voice was completely drowned by the sea.

I started over the rock toward him, and then I realised that only one leg was working. My other leg was no use to me. Every time I moved I got a terrible pain round my hip. So I got down on the rock, and I dragged myself across to Aldo. I got my arms behind his shoulders and I heaved him clear of the water but I couldn't get him any further.

The tide came in and sucked at him, and I held on in a tug of war with the water, and he didn't move. He was cold, but he wasn't *dead* cold . . . there was life in him. There had to be life in him, for I wasn't going to die alone.

That stuck in my head, and then it changed. I wasn't going to die. Aldo wasn't going to die. Not after all that.

The sea was rising. I got hold of him, and I dragged and I dragged. I could only move him a tiny fraction at a time, up the wet slithery rock with the tide breaking round us.

I couldn't move him any more. I had pulled him up the rock as far as I could and the whole of my bad leg, and that side of my body where the leg was hurt had gone numb and I could feel very little. I lay back against Aldo and I was getting sleepy and you can't get sleepy or you die.

But I wasn't going to die.

There were people there. Somebody pulled me away from Aldo and laid me on the rock and later still I was up in the air on a stretcher thing and there was a terrible whirring noise and Aldo was in the cab of the helicopter with me but he was lying still and he couldn't talk.

We went whirring up in the air, over the cliff, and I bet we disturbed more gulls than the old Spaniard ever did!

"I'm giving you an injection," the man said.

118

It didn't hurt. All I remember is wondering what Orla would say when I told her I'd been up in a helicopter, and why stupid old Owen Leary never caught on about the gull.

Thirteen

"You should have been dead," Orla said, kicking her heels against Egg's wall. "I bet I would have been dead, if it was me. You were dead lucky, Nora Mullan."

I didn't think it was dead lucky to be hopping around in a plaster cast on a pair of crutches after rescuing somebody I didn't even know from drowning, but she did.

Typical Orla!

I didn't much mind. I let her talk on. I was all right. All the talk was that my father would get the job at the Field Centre, though he hadn't had final word yet. That was what Stella had to go to town for, to get him, and she had taken Chris so that my father could speak to him on his own. I could have stayed in our house and never been half killed.

I came out of it all right. Even Aldo was all right. The one who wasn't all right was Brendan.

"Look at him!" Orla said, scornfully.

Brendan was down on the shore, alone. That is the way he is mostly, since the big row. Mrs. Egg says he's not to mix with the Ballyhannis School boys again, in case he gets them into more trouble. If you ask me it was Damien who caused the real trouble, but he got off with a pasting from his father, which is nothing new in the Hughes' household. I will never forgive Damien for scaring Chris with his lies about Erk. Brendan only made his gun for showing off, he would never have shot Erk, but making the gun got him into trouble with the police, and put all the grown ups against him.

I watched him turn and walk along toward the harbour. He was slouching in his usual way, but then something came running at him from the sluice pipe, and he brightened up.

It was Erk.

He was easily pleased, with only Erk to talk to.

"Come on," I said. "Let's go and talk to Brendan."

"I'm not allowed to," said Orla. "My Mammy doesn't let me."

I wobbled off down the beach on my crutches, alone. I went because I was sorry for him and the trouble he had made for himself. He was being blamed for everything that had gone wrong, which was very convenient for all of us. I went down to the shore to talk to him because I was sorry for him, but most of all I went because I knew that if I didn't go, crutches and all, nobody else was going to.

A Selected List of Fiction from Mammoth

The prices shown below were correct at the time of going to press.

☐	416 13972 8	**Why the Whales Came**	Michael Murpurgo	£2.50
☐	7497 0034 3	**My Friend Walter**	Michael Murpurgo	£2.50
☐	7497 0035 1	**The Animals of Farthing Wood**	Colin Dann	£2.99
☐	416 01366	**I Am David**	Anne Holm	£2.50
☐	7497 0139 0	**Snow Spider**	Jenny Nimmo	£2.50
☐	7497 0140 4	**Emlyn's Moon**	Jenny Nimmo	£2.25
☐	7497 0344 X	**The Haunting**	Margaret Mahy	£2.25
☐	416 96850 3	**Catalogue of the Universe**	Margaret Mahy	£1.95
☐	7497 0051 3	**My Friend Flicka**	Mary O'Hara	£2.99
☐	7497 0079 3	**Thunderhead**	Mary O'Hara	£2.99
☐	7497 0219 2	**Green Grass of Wyoming**	Mary O'Hara	£2.99
☐	416 13772 9	**Rival Games**	Michael Hardcastle	£1.99
☐	416 13212 X	**Mascot**	Michael Hardcastle	£1.99
☐	7497 0126 9	**Half a Team**	Michael Hardcastle	£1.99
☐	416 08812 0	**The Whipping Boy**	Sid Fleischman	£1.99
☐	7497 0033 5	**The Lives of Christopher Chant**	Diana Wynne-Jones	£2.50
☐	7497 0164 1	**A Visit to Folly Castle**	Nina Beechcroft	£2.25

All these books are available at your bookshop or newsagent, or can be ordered direct from the publisher. Just tick the titles you want and fill in the form below.

Mandarin Paperbacks, Cash Sales Department, PO Box 11, Falmouth, Cornwall TR10 9EN.

Please send cheque or postal order, no currency, for purchase price quoted and allow the following for postage and packing:

UK   80p for the first book, 20p for each additional book ordered to a maximum charge of £2.00.

BFPO   80p for the first book, 20p for each additional book.

Overseas   £1.50 for the first book, £1.00 for the second and 30p for each additional book
including Eire   thereafter.

NAME (Block letters) ....

ADDRESS ....

....

....